Claimed by the Alpha

A book in the Sanctuary Series

Book One

J. Raven Wilde

Editing services provided by Kelly Hartigan at XterraWeb (editing.xterraweb.com). Published by Twisted Crow Press, LLC

Published by Twisted Crow Press, LLC

www.twistedcrowpress.com

ISBN: 979-8-9906871-1-0

Other Books by J. Raven Wilde

Standalone Novels

His Orders

Hot and Steamy Series

In Hot Pursuit

Hot Rod

One Hot Weekend

Falling For Series

Falling for the Rancher

Falling for the Cowboy

The Mummy's Curse Mini-Series

The Mummy's Curse Vol 1

The Sorcerer's Curse Vol 2

The Curse of Anubis Vol 3

The Mummy's Curse Mini-Series Box Set

Sanctuary Series

Claimed by the Alpha

The Omega and the Witch

The Rogue and the Rebel

Deerskin Peaks Series

Claimed by the Bear

Taming the Wildcat

1

Gemma

This day could not have gotten any better. I had filled out twenty-three applications within a few days. Four of which had responded. I went in for each interview, but afterward, I was told they had found someone else to fill the position, they weren't certain they could hire someone who moved around a lot, or I hadn't held a job longer than a month. It's understandable. Though I had zigzagged across the map starting from near the northeast coastline, I would only put the last few employers on my application.

This morning, I received a call to come in this afternoon for another interview, and I was nervous I wouldn't get this job either. It was hard being on the run. I didn't have any kind of stable employment history and no permanent address. I had stolen some money from my father and spent a few hundred dollars to buy a used car from a friend of mine, and then I used the remaining cash to travel around the country in hopes that I would be safe.

After four months of moving from one run-down motel room to the next, my money was almost gone. It was time to see about getting a job here in Oregon. I only wanted something that was going to be temporary, but I was not telling my hopefully future employers that. I needed something that would help me put a little money away to afford relocating again. After I had filled out every job application in the surrounding areas where they had posted help wanted signs, as well as answering most of the employment ads in the newspaper, I was becoming desperate for just about anything now. There *must* be something out there for me.

However, I didn't want to work for any law firm or office; I wanted to hide who I was and avoid running into anyone who would discover my identity by doing a background search. But I found myself stuck, broke, and desperate. There were two ads left in the help wanted section that I had not bothered looking into; one was for a secretary job at a law firm, and the other one looked to be for the same type of job, but I could not tell who the company was or what they did. Oddly, they were the only ones who asked for me to come in for an interview. It had been five days since I turned in my last application, but with no response, I was elated when they called.

I crossed my fingers and whispered a silent plea in hopes they wouldn't need to run a background check or ask for references, which I did not have. I didn't want to explain that I was on the run because of werewolf politics. It was hard enough being the alpha's daughter, but I was one of the few females who unfortunately survived and ended up being human. Although, being a human had its perks when on the run; I wouldn't be detected by any other were that stumbled into the wrong territory. As long as nobody knew my real identity, I was safe.

I stepped out of my car and entered the building. From the outside, it appeared to be a large warehouse with three loading docks that were currently empty. When I walked in through the doors, I was greeted by the scent of cinnamon, with a hint of something sweet. After taking a couple of quick sniffs, I was able to determine that it was apples. It was like walking into a bakery, not an office building, and I could picture cinnamon rolls and apple pie sitting in a display case. My stomach grumbled in response. I only had a granola bar for breakfast, and it was already past lunchtime.

I stood just inside the doorway, looking straight at a walnut-colored desk roughly ten feet away. Sadly, there were no pastries to be found. Over to my left were five simple brown leather chairs in the small waiting area. Over to my right was a small walnut-colored wooden table that matched the desk, with a handful of brochures and business cards, both of which read "McKinney's Shipping and Storage." I assumed that was where I was since I still didn't know what kind of business had called me in to interview with them.

As I approached the desk and took in the space around the room, I didn't see anyone there. Glancing around the large room, I noticed two doors on my right, a door behind the desk, and a door and hallway to my left. Two plastic ficus trees stood behind the desk, one in each corner and an occasional framed picture of castles from faraway lands hung around the office, one picture to a wall.

"Hello?" I called out in a normal voice, afraid to raise it any higher.

My body trembled with nervousness, scared that I was in the wrong place. It didn't help that no one was here to greet me. My mind was screaming to run, but my feet stayed planted where I stood. Between the plant life, the dark brown furniture, and the tan walls, the space seemed warm and inviting, yet a cool chill, that had nothing to do with the air conditioning, ran through me, sending up warning signals.

Seconds later, the door behind the desk opened, and I was greeted by a glistening white smile attached to a tall muscular male body. His eyes were golden brown, like the color of warm honey. His hair, a shade darker than his eyes, was trimmed short and combed back. He wore a black buttoned-up shirt, sleeves rolled up to his elbows, gray slacks, and expensive dress shoes that looked like something I would find in my father's closet. He also wore a watch I was sure cost three times the price of his shoes. Anyone who could afford those things had money to spend, and I silently hoped that this job would pay well and that I would be hired.

Inwardly, I groaned. He was handsome. So much so that I stared at him, dumbfounded.

"Hello, Gemma Smith?" He greeted me with a warm voice that made me smile. I took a deep breath as I felt my temperature go up a few degrees.

I nodded, afraid I'd trip over my tongue. I'm such an idiot. Potentially, he could be my boss and I'm already drooling.? Snap out of it, Gem.

"I'm John Trenton," he said, offering me his hand. I shook it as he continued, "Thank you for agreeing to interview with me today. As you can see, I'm the only one here. We're a small, family-owned company, you could say. So, it's typical that there aren't too many people working here on Fridays."

He opened the door, holding it and motioning me to cross the threshold in front of him. I smiled nervously as I obliged him, stopping just a few feet inside a small office with a desk befitting a secretary adorned with a computer, two sorting trays, a cup with pens, and a small plant. But what really caught my eye was the large piles of papers covering the desk and filing cabinets.

I quickly followed him through another door that led into a large office with the same warm earth tones in the décor and furniture. The furniture looked more comfortable to sit in compared to the waiting area. He sat down behind a large wooden desk as he motioned for me to sit in one of the chairs in front of it.

"I gathered from your application that you don't have any clerical experience?" he asked with raised eyebrows.

I swallowed too hard, trying to push my stomach down that was stirring due to being so nervous. I only listed a few of my previous jobs however short-lived they were. How could I tell him my situation without telling him too much or without sounding desperate?

I cleared my throat and took a deep breath before I began. "I don't have much experience working in an office, no, but I have no problem answering a phone and I'm capable of using a computer. And I can type really well. I'm not sure how many words a minute, but I can type."

I watched him nod at my answer as he looked over the application. He glanced up at me and said, "Tell me a bit about yourself. I see that you move around a lot?"

Here we go, the question I dread answering. You would think that I would be able to come up with a perfectly good explanation by now, but so far, I haven't thought of anything that was beneficial in securing me employment.

"Um, well, I … I am young and still trying to find myself. I love to travel."

"I can see that." He chuckled. "Do you think you will be staying here for a few months?"

"If I can find a job, that could be a possibility."

"Well, what I'm looking for is someone who could answer phones, file, take messages and leave them here on the desk, which I'm sure you could follow through with. Keep things organized. I also need someone to type up clients' information and record their schedules into an online form, print out invoices. It's simple work. There are notes on the desktop, which are self-explanatory."

"I can certainly manage that."

"When can you start?"

"I can start tomorrow," I smiled brightly.

He laughed and said, "Tomorrow is Saturday, and we don't usually have anyone in the office on the weekends. But, how would Monday sound?"

"Yes, Monday is great." I beamed.

"You'll occasionally see the boss, Aiden McKinney coming and going from time to time. Don't let him scare you."

"Thank you, Mr. Trenton." I stood up and shook his hand a little too firmly. My face hurt from smiling. I didn't think my smile could get any bigger.

2

Gemma

There wasn't anyone in the office my first day though, oddly, the door was unlocked. The phone only rang twice, and both times it sounded like the same person who told me they would call back another time. I wasn't sure what I was supposed to do exactly, so I made myself familiar with the layout of my small workspace, including the contents inside my desk and on the computer, which didn't have much in either. My desk held a couple of blank legal pads, paperclips, pens, and a couple of thumbtacks. The computer was even sparser than the desk as it only had the basic calculator and a Word document for typing letters. It didn't even have solitaire or any other games, which made me think this was more of a real work space and not much leisure time was allowed.

I turned in my chair to stare at the three four-drawer filing cabinets that stood behind me like a large metal wall. At the end of one stood a table with a four-tier sorting tray that overflowed with papers. I walked over to it and thumbed through the papers, looking for anything that might tell me what they were for; were they supposed to be filed, or were they for something else entirely? I wasn't sure, but I made use of my time to sort through them.

Hours had passed, and I had turned the overflow of papers into neat, orderly stacks on my desk and on top of the filing cabinet. A tall man in a business suit casually walked in through the doors and stopped a few feet in front of my desk. He was much taller than Mr. Trenton with dark chocolate-brown hair and a clean-shaven square jaw. He seemed to suck out the oxygen in the room as his muscular physique devoured the space in which he resided. I was finding it hard to concentrate, and my heart sped up. I wanted him to rip my clothes off and devour me right here.

I shook my head to clear my dirty thoughts. I could feel his eyes boring into me as I placed a file folder back into the bottom drawer of the third cabinet and stood to meet his gaze again as I took in a deep breath. He didn't look happy. Although, having ran into someone you didn't know, thumbing through your files, while stacks of papers containing important information were spread out across the desk for anyone to see was not a great first impression. I could understand why he would appear unhappy. Something about him just now made my hair stand up, sending warning signals to my brain to take precaution.

I cleared my throat a few times, trying to push my stomach back down. How could a man excite me and scare me at the same time?

"Hi, I'm Gemma Smith. I was hired yesterday by a Mr. Trenton—" I began cheerfully, but he cut me off before I could finish.

"Were you now? And what on earth are you doing, Miss. Smith?" he said in a stern voice making my body shiver with nervousness.

His voice was deep, but that wasn't what made the hairs on my skin stand up. I had looked into his eyes and noticed the subtle changes of color from green to gold. He was a were, but which species, I couldn't tell. I knew I was going to be in trouble and diverted my gaze to his chest. I couldn't have him mad at me, and then find out who I was. He sniffed once and I knew he could decipher that I was a human, which meant I had to play it cool and not let him know that I was aware of what he was.

J. Raven Wilde

I tried to hide my nervousness, but my voice cracked, giving me away. "Um, I ... I wasn't sure since there wasn't anyone here ... when he told me to be here ... so I saw this stack of papers and decided to file them." I waved my hand toward the stack of papers, never taking my eyes off him.

I tried looking anywhere but in his eyes. Making direct eye contact with him again while he was showing me this much irritation and the need for him to shift would be a bad judgment call on my part.

He didn't say anything more and strode into his office, slamming the door behind him. A few seconds later, I heard him shouting at someone he must have called on his phone.

"I'm sorry," I mumbled, wishing the person on the other end could hear me. I took another look at my desk and swore under my breath at the stupidity I had shown. I had never worked at an office before. Every job I had taken these past few months was either cleaning motel rooms or waiting on tables. My father never allowed me to find employment, so I was lacking in the work experience department. There was only one job he had in mind for me and it was the reason why I had to leave.

"—I told you not to hire another woman, yet you ignored me. Why?" he shouted.

I knew who he was talking to just from listening to his half of the conversation. Honestly, I wasn't trying to listen in, but it was rather hard not to with him shouting.

"—you're right, I did need someone here to help me, but I told you exactly what I was looking for when I put you in charge of hiring my staff for me."

I felt bad for myself and for Mr. Trenton. Though, I felt worse for myself as I needed the money. I had twenty-three dollars left of the twenty-five hundred dollars I set out with, and that wasn't counting the extra change I made doing odd jobs, all of which was gone. Twenty-three dollars wasn't going to last me too much longer. Rent was paid up for the month, but I was running low on food and other essentials. I stood there staring at the desk, battling myself on whether I should just pick up the papers and pile them neatly on the corner of the desk and quit my job or wait out the fury that was still brewing in the office next to me. I thought it was best just to leave.

3

Aiden

I stormed into my office, slamming the door behind me and pulling out my cell phone.

"Hey, boss." John's voice came out a little too cheerful, and I growled lowly, so he would know that I wasn't sharing the same sentiment.

"I told you not to hire another woman, yet you ignored me. Why?" I shouted.

"You needed someone at the office."

If he wasn't my half-brother and the only omega in my territory, I would rip his throat out for his disobedience.

"You're right, I did need someone here to help me, but I told you, exactly what I was looking for when I put you in charge of hiring my staff for me."

"Right, and we're losing guys right and left because you're too stubborn to do what you need to do. I'm not hiring another male so you can bite his head off."

"I don't need a human male with dominant characteristics," I sneered.

"Why you need a female. And you need her. It's a win-win."

"I don't see how you get that."

"That's because you're in denial. You need to smell her again."

My chest rumbled with a low growl. I did smell her. She reeked of fear, arousal, and something else that I couldn't distinguish at that very moment. "Is that why you hired her?"

"She sounded desperate and in need of help. So, I offered her a job. It's up to you to figure out which *job* she's to accept."

I sighed knowing where he was going with this. My pack was suffering because of me. I snarled at the thought of my brother trying to help me find a mate. That wasn't what I asked him to help me with, but he was my second in command.

I pressed end, tossed the phone onto my desk, and stormed out. I watched her drop a stack of papers, creating a bigger mess on her desk. A hand flew up to her chest as she let out a gasp. I scared her. Good. She needs to be afraid of the big bad wolf. My chest rumbled as my wolf agreed.

I stood there, watching her for a moment. She was frozen in place. I guess she was waiting on me to bark an order. Would she obey if I did? My eyes roamed over her body. She had on a short-sleeved flower print cotton dress that hugged her curvy frame in all the right places. Once my eyes moved up to her face, she licked her lips and my cock twitched. Her heart was racing.

I took in a breath and smelled fear. She refused to make eye contact. Maybe that was a good thing. I would bet that if she looked up at me now, her scent of fear would thicken. I wondered how that would also affect the small hint of her arousal I picked up. My wolf was stirring as much as my cock was.

I took in another whiff, trying to figure out what it was John said I should smell. It was there—faint, but there. John was never wrong when it came to smelling things out. That was what made him the perfect second in command. Maybe I could keep her around long enough to find out what it was.

"You can work for the remainder of the week, but, for future reference, don't lay out my clients' personal information all over your desk for anyone who walked in here to read."

I didn't give her time to reply. I quickly turned on my heel and strode back into my office and straight to my desk. From what I could see, John didn't leave a file for her or her application on my desk.

I glanced over at my door. I could hear her moving around. Who was she and why did she interest John enough to put her in front of me like this? He would never disobey me. I had a handful of women work for me. I made sure each one of them was married or only looking for temporary work. I didn't need a distraction. No, I needed a mate. My pack was suffering because I hadn't taken one. I had failed them as their alpha.

4

Gemma

The week seemed to fly by, thankfully, and we seemed to avoid one another. Mostly, he stayed in his office. The only time he left was when I took my lunch break in the small employee break room. Occasionally, the phone rang, and I had to send it to his office, but we never spoke. I hadn't seen Mr. Trenton since the day he hired me, and I silently hoped he hadn't been fired because of me. I did run into a few other employees, all males, but none of them spoke to me; they simply smiled at me as they continued walking to wherever they were going.

Come Friday, as Mr. Trenton had promised, there was no one around, including Mr. McKinney. When I approached my desk, there was an envelope with my name on it, and inside was my check for this week's pay. It was a generous amount as it included an couple extra hundred dollars more than what I should be paid. I'm sure he did that to push me into finding another job. I selfishly thought that he could've added a few more dollars for having yelled at me the way he did, but I wasn't going to be greedy. I was happy to take what he offered. Putting the check in my purse, I turned back around and walked out the door, heading back to my dingy room to continue scanning the want ads.

While waiting in the laundry room for my clothes to wash, I wandered over to the bulletin board to look for employment. It had to be fate that I found an advertisement for a catering server position hanging on it. I called the number on the ad and was told to pick up a uniform that day as the position was for a party being held at the golf club tomorrow night. The event would last about four hours, and I would be paid one hundred and fifty dollars after it was over.

The catering office wasn't hard to find, and they seemed like nice people, especially compared to Mr. McKinney. I filled out the necessary paperwork and walked away with two uniforms, and the address of the party on Saturday night. They also asked me if I would be interested in working at another party next Friday and Saturday night at the same place, and I agreed.

*****

I left my room early so I had plenty of time to find the golf club. I showed up fifteen minutes early, which impressed my supervisor. She allowed me to walk around the room and help set up tables and chairs. It wasn't long before everyone began to show up and finished setting the last of the food trays. Minutes later, the party attendees began to arrive.

I had waited tables a few times at a couple of restaurants, so it wasn't hard carrying a tray of food or drinks around the room. What was hard was being hit on. Generally, I didn't find the simple flirt hard to manage, but one guy was being particularly relentless. He was an older guy, probably in his fifties, balding, and wearing cowboy boots with his cheap suit.

He seemed to wait until I passed by him to say something to me. And each time, the comments went from slight flirting to something close to sexual harassment, which had me avoiding his part of the room entirely, making it hard to do my job.

I walked out of the kitchen and back into the room and about dropped my tray when I spotted the old guy talking to Mr. McKinney.

"Oh, just perfect," I grumbled under my breath. I went about walking half of the room, far away from those two, not even looking in their direction.

Someone tapped my shoulder. "Excuse me, Miss, but I feel stood up," said a familiar voice. It was the old guy. "It seems that you have been ignoring me."

I tried not to show my annoyance and turned around and showed him a smile that wasn't genuine. "I'm sorry, sir, but as you can see, I'm working. I can't stand around and chat."

"I can see that. I could put you to work," he added, and his eyes glazed over as he raked them over my body suggestively.

I felt like hurling in my mouth, but instead, I politely excused myself and made my way back to the kitchen, walking as briskly as possible, leaving him to smirk by himself.

There wasn't anyone else in the kitchen when I sat the tray down onto the counter. I closed my eyes, tilted my head back and sighed, willing this night to move by a little faster. I reached up to massage my temples when a rough hand grabbed my arm and pulled me outside. I stumbled a few times, trying my best to keep up with him as he took long strides. The grip on my arm was starting to bruise, and I cried out, trying to pull out of his painful grasp.

"Ow! You're hurting me," I said through gritted teeth. I didn't want to draw an audience, or I would've shouted.

We made it just outside the tall wooden fence that ran around the backside of the golf clubhouse when he slammed me up against the fence. Tears stung my eyes, but my breath hitched, and I coiled back as he got into my face.

"Just what the hell do you think you're doing?"

His breath was hot against my skin, sending a fire roaring throughout my body. Ugh, my traitorous body. I was scared of him at this moment, but I was more turned on when he shoved me against the fence and invaded my space with his masculinity. He smelled like his office, apples and cinnamon, but with a hint of the outdoors. Why did he have to smell so good?

"I'm working," I said with a shaky voice. "You fired me, remember?"

He stepped back a few feet, and I glanced up to see his nostrils flaring as he took in a deep breath and released it. The moonlight shone on his face, and I saw a slight change of color in his eyes. I didn't want to piss him—a were—off. He glared at me, intent. I wasn't sure what it was that I had done wrong now. When he fired me, was I supposed to leave town? How was I to know he would show up here of all places.

I flinched as he raised an arm, but he didn't strike me, only pointed back toward the clubhouse. "That man, the one you were talking to? Stay away from him," he said with a sneer. He leaned in closer, getting within inches of my face, and said quietly, "Do you hear me?"

I was starting to get frustrated now with him telling me what I should and shouldn't do. Who was that guy to him? And why did I need to stay away from him? I needed to leave town now, but I couldn't. Not yet. I needed to try and save up a little and figure out where else I could go.

"Wha ... what am I supposed to do then? I need to go back to work. I need the money."

I flinched again as he reached into his pocket, pulling out his wallet. He thumbed through the bills, pulled a couple free, and then roughly stuffed them into the front pocket of my vest before stepping back again. "For your troubles."

I started once to make a snide comment. Troubles, yes, I agree with staying out of trouble, but I'm going to be in trouble if I didn't get back to work. "Am I supposed to just leave and not finish my shift?"

"Did you not hear a word I just said?" he growled.

"Yes, I heard *every* word you said, but have you forgotten? You fired me. You're no longer my boss," I retorted. "We're not family, we are *not* dating, we are *certainly* not married. So, the way I see it, you don't have the right to tell me what to do."

I knew I should not have snapped, but I couldn't help it. He pissed me off, starting from the first moment he stormed in the office that day and began yelling at me before firing me. Now he was adding to it, starting with bruising my arm and ordering me around. I reached up and rubbed my arm, wincing as the pain started to settle in where he grabbed and pulled me. I gave him a soured look. He didn't need to be so rough.

His nostrils flared again, and he shut his eyes. I could tell he was fighting the urge to shift, and I wasn't helping him any by making him mad. Sometimes, I just couldn't control the words that came out of my mouth or the tone that delivered them.

I took a deep breath to calm my own temper. "I'm sorry," I said quietly. "I'll just grab my purse and phone a cab, then I'll be out of your sight for good."

He opened his eyes and reached for my arm again, and I pulled back, causing him to let out a growl. It was a loud rumble in his chest, and my heart jumped at the sound. "I'm sorry, but you hurt me. If you want me to go somewhere, simply tell me. I'm not a ragdoll, I'm a human being, and I bruise easily. You don't have to grab me so hard," I said assuredly.

"You'll take my car. If you follow me, my driver can take you anywhere you need to go," he said through his teeth.

"And my purse?" I placed my hands upon my hips, standing firmly in place, showing him, I wasn't going to be ignored.

"I'll go get it, but *only* after you're in my car." He motioned toward a black sedan that was waiting by the curb in the parking lot. I watched as someone got into the driver's side and started the car. Mr. McKinney opened the door for me, allowing me to get in, and then leaned down to say something, "This is Andrew, he's my driver. Your purse, what does it look like?"

His closeness had my heart beating so hard that I almost didn't hear what he said. I shook my head and stuttered. "Oh … ah … yes, my, my purse. I-It's black and small with three zippers and a silver "R" on it," I said, trying to picture it in my mind. I couldn't remember if I had switched my purses out and mentally crossed my fingers that I told him the right one. I didn't want him coming back to the car really pissed off at me.

I sat in silence, waiting for what felt like an eternity, and when the door opened, he got in and handed me my purse. I gave a half smile and gladly took it from him.

"Andrew," he said to the driver, and Andrew put the car in drive and pulled out of the parking lot. I gave him my address, and Mr. McKinney cocked his head, as if what I said was interesting. "That's where you're staying, that old, run-down motel?"

"Yes. And it isn't so run-down. Besides, it was all I could afford at the time and all I could find," I said, trying not to snap. He grumbled and started to say something, but I cut him off. "Look, I'm fine staying there. It's only temporary. Not like I could afford anything nicer." I said that last sentence a bit sharper, hoping he would understand that I was still not happy with him keeping me from making an income.

"Andrew, take us home."

"Wait, what? You're taking me back to my room, right?" my voice squeaked.

"No," he said, as if our conversation was done and I was not to argue.

I started to open my mouth to tell him to take me back to my place, but he turned his gaze toward me and glared. His chest rumbled with a low growl, and his eyes held a yellow ring around the iris, and I knew that it was best to just sit back in the seat and be silent. Avoid eye contact at all cost.

I did just that, crossing my arms and releasing a huff. It was all I could do not to give him an earful, but I had learned quickly around my father, the alpha were of the East

Coast wolf pack, that you never look a were in the eyes when they're changing or on the verge of changing. You never argued with one, nor did you raise your voice unless you are ready to fight them. Raising the tone of your voice only makes matters bad, but eye contact when you were shouting was worse. It was as if you were challenging them. And tonight, I was breaking all those rules.

I glared out the window, hoping that he could sense the anger rolling off me. My father would've backhanded me if he were here. But he wasn't, and I was no longer going to let him control my life. Aiden might be hot and very short-tempered, but I could dish some of that right back—forget about him being a were. I was tired of men always thinking they could control me.

5

Aiden

We sat in silence, thankfully, on the ride back to my estate. It was a good thing she stopped talking when she did. My wolf was so close to coming out. When I had pushed her into the fence, gotten close to her, and inhaled her scent, there was a hint of fear that was covered up with the scent of her arousal. It stirred my own so much that I grew hard. But there was something else there I still couldn't quite place, yet it was calling to my wolf, wanting me to shift to get a better smell.

The tension was so thick in my car I was beginning to suffocate. I could sense she was pissed off at me right now, and it wasn't helping me. I sighed. Maybe it might not be safe for her to come back home with me until I could figure out who she was. I had never had a hard time controlling myself around a woman before, and she was being more than difficult. I was also finding it hard to suppress the urge to shift when I was around her. My wolf had never shown any interest in a woman before either. So why now? What made her so special?

"Andrew, slight change of plans. We're going to take Miss Smith back to her place."

"Yes, sir," Andrew replied.

I glanced over at Gemma. Her body seemed to relax when she heard this news.

"Thank you," she said.

That seemed to help the tension die down some. I continued to look out the window, focusing on remaining calm. Her scent was stirring my wolf again. Even though we were sitting as far away from one another as possible, I could tell her emotions were all over the place. I chanced another glance at her. She was staring out the window. The faint glow of the passing streets light lit up her face, and I noticed a hint of a smile, curving her luscious rosy lips.

Sighing, I turned my gaze away, trying to ignore the throbbing bulge in my pants. I was trying not to find any attractive qualities in her and silently cursed John for having me really look at her. She was a distraction. A very curious one.

I glanced out the window again and watched the scenery change as we arrived in the impoverished side of town. When we pulled into the parking lot, I glanced over at the sign for this establishment and took in the building standing before us. Surely this couldn't be where she said she was staying? It looked like every health hazard imaginable.

I wanted to ask Andrew if we were at the right place, but I knew that would be an insult. Instead, I looked over at Gemma who was now reaching for the door handle. Gently, I placed my hand over hers, causing her to flinch.

"This is where you're staying?"

"Yes." She sat up straighter, holding her head high. "I told you this already. It's only temporary."

"Yes, so you've said. I knew this place was run-down, but I didn't know it was a death trap."

"Mr. McKinney, please. I'm okay with staying here."

My wolf was scratching at me to take her home. For once tonight, I was agreeing with him. It would damage her pride, apparently, but I would have a hard time letting her stay here a moment longer. Distractions be damned.

"My place, Andrew," I said as I waited for her reaction.

She tried to turn the handle, but the locks were still secured. "You are going to let me out of this car, right now," she shouted.

"There has to be fifty health code violations. Five just from looking at it. I will not be the one at fault should something happen to you."

"Oh, now you come around," she snapped. "I thought you were so quick to get rid of me so, why should you even bother to care what happens to me? You don't even know me, but I can tell you one thing, mister, I can take care of myself." Her eyes went wide as if she realized her mistake in taking that tone with me. Would she still shout at me if she knew *who* I was?

My nostrils flared, and I took in a few deep breaths to calm myself. Maybe I should've just let her out at that dump and been done with her. As an alpha, I wasn't used to having someone acting so defiantly. Typically, anyone who did yell at me knew right away that it was at their own peril. It was also my job as an alpha to take care of others.

I let out a low growl as a warning, and immediately, she looked down at the floor. She scooted back into her seat, pulling her legs up into her chest and wrapping her arms around her. It was a sign of submission, and I was wondering if she *did* know who I was. That only piqued my curiosity even more.

When we pulled into the driveway of my estate, I watched her reaction. It was just as I expected it would be—surprised. My estate was immense, but it wasn't all mine. Though, as alpha, I had the right to claim it as mine, as the alpha before me had done, I decided to share it with my pack. Currently, most of them were in wolf form, out running through the hundreds of acres of woodland area surrounding the house.

I stepped out of the car first and waited on her to follow before escorting her inside. "I'll take you to your room," I said, walking up the stairs.

"Wait, *my* room?"

I stopped and turned around slowly. "Well, you don't want it to be *my* room." I smirked at her negative reaction before continuing to climb the stairs to the first floor, turning right, and walking down the east wing. I stopped at one of the doors and glanced at her as she approached me, stopping within a few feet.

"This will be your room for now. You are not to go outside under *any* circumstances. Do *not* leave without telling me. It's for your own safety that you adhere to these simple rules." I watched her sigh before opening the door to let her walk in, but she just stood there, glaring at me. *Making eye contact again. Stubborn woman.*

"Unless you care to join me in my room across the hall here?" I gestured toward the door directly across from hers.

I smirked as she stepped inside her room and slammed the door in my face.

I took in a deep breath and held it for a few seconds, releasing it in a loud sigh. Her scent still lingered near her door. *I need to go for a run.* I stared at her door for a moment, listening in. The sounds of her footsteps receding away from the door was what I needed to hear. Nodding, I briskly made my way down the stairs and through the back of the house, stripping my clothes off just as I got outside the kitchen door, and shifted.

6

Gemma

I sighed, loudly, as I took in the room. I needed to figure out what I was going to do with this situation I seemed to have put myself in. I needed my space, my freedom. My father kept me locked up in the house, forbidding me to go anywhere. Once I hit puberty, I was forbidden from ever leaving my room. A month before I turned eighteen, he told me he was giving me to Mack, the son of his second in command, in hopes of strengthening the bond of our packs. Since we were now engaged, he allowed me to date Mack.

Mack was a few years older than me. He was tall and muscular, yet I just wasn't attracted to him. Our first two dates went rather nice, but on our third date, I started to see what kind of person he was. He thought that since we were engaged to be married that he could go ahead and consummate the marriage a little early.

I fought him and fought hard, and after I escaped, I made it home and showed my father the horrible bruises and scratches covering my face and body. His only response was for me to get used to it as that was how wolves should treat their disobedient wives.

I had never been so hurt or angry in my whole life as I was that day. My tutor told me that my father should've cherished me. Yet he didn't. Women born with were DNA, who actually survived, were considered rare. Women who could be turned and survive were even rarer. He thought that since I survived and had the werewolf gene I could bear him many strong grandsons.

There was only one problem. I wasn't sticking around long enough to let this become my life. I had planned my escape for months with the help of my tutor. Later that night, I escaped, sneaking out of my room when I knew my father wasn't there, and snatched money from his desk. Being an alpha, he must've trusted that none of his pack would steal from him. He didn't think about what I would possibly do, knowing how scared of him I was.

As the memories hit me, I started to sweat. My heart raced, and I was finding it hard to breathe. I needed some air. I cracked the door open a few inches and peeked out. Opened it a few more inches wider, I ducked my head out, and looked around. I paused to listen. Nothing. *Guess he left?*

I went downstairs and into the kitchen, walking carefully and quietly, before stepping outside. I didn't want Mr. Grouchy Wolf to bark and growl at me for leaving my room. I would just have to let him know that I wasn't going to be held prisoner. Although, that was all I would divulge on that matter.

A few more feet away from the house, I stopped and closed my eyes, taking in a deep breath. The air was slightly chilly, but it was crisp and clean. I smiled as I sat down on the grass. It was so quiet that I could fall asleep out here. I leaned my head back and peered up at the stars. *What a view.* I never really paid much attention to them honestly. In a way, I was mesmerized.

Several minutes passed by and I could feel the chill nipping at my arms. I didn't want to go back inside. I took in another breath when I heard a deep growl. Damn! Opening my eyes, I found myself within a few yards of a large chestnut-colored wolf. Knowing my luck, this would be Aiden McKinney. And from the sounds of his snarling, he was pissed.

Sanctuary: Claimed by the Alpha

7

Aiden

I stepped out of the tree line and was making my way back to the house when I spotted someone sitting outside a few feet from the back door.

Her.

I inched my way forward, snapping my jowls, snarling and growling. I was furious that she would ignore the rules that I gave her and risk her life. I wasn't the only wolf out here tonight, but being the alpha, I was one that could control myself in my wolf form right now.

Her eyes went wide when I took off running toward her, but she tripped, falling face-first into the hard ground. I leaped up onto her back, and she flattened herself on the ground. I could smell it now. She had wolf running through her blood. My wolf needed to rut, to claim her as ours. I knew there was something about her that I couldn't place, but now that I had shifted, I could smell it, and my wolf found her intoxicating.

Mine! The words that kept running through my mind, making me delirious. I leaned in near her ear and growled, snapping my jowls, careful not to nip her skin.

She stopped moving long enough for me to come to my senses. I couldn't claim her right here, not in this form. She whimpered as I grabbed her shirt collar with my teeth, and I growled as I began to pull her toward the door.

"Okay, okay, I'll go back inside," she said.

I moved off her, following her inside the house, growling every few feet and nipping at her heels to show her I was serious. Just as we made it into the east wing, she opened her door and rushed inside, slamming the door behind her.

Clever girl.

I forced myself to change and then stormed inside her room. Her eyes went big as she stared at my large prick as it grew harder with each step, I took toward her. She didn't make it easy for me since she was on her bed, scooting as close as she could to her headboard, making her look every bit like defenseless prey.

I snarled as I grabbed her ankle, pulling her down toward me, and laid on top of her, pinning her hands and legs down with my own.

She slammed her eyes shut and whimpered, "I'm sorry, I'm sorry. Please, don't hurt me."

"I gave specific instructions *not* to go outside, did I not?" I growled, inches from her face.

"Yes, and I'm sorry, I just needed some air. I wasn't trying to leave."

I growled when she began to squirm, trying to free herself. She was rubbing herself against me, unknowingly, I'm sure, but made me ache even more. I was fighting the urge to take her.

"If you don't be still, woman, I am going to lose the fight and take you here and now."

She stilled, and I eased up off her enough to look into her eyes.

"Look at me," I said quietly.

She opened her eyes but refused to make eye contact.

"*Look* at me," I snapped, and she complied.

"How is it that you smell like a wolf? Do you belong to someone? Are you mated to another, or are you pregnant?"

Her eyes went wide, and I could see the tears forming. She closed her eyes, and the tears fell. She shook her head, "No, not like that. My … my father … he's a wolf, like you."

I grunted. Not what I wanted to hear, but it explained her scent. "Where are you from and why are you here in my territory? I would've known if one of my wolves had a female that survived into adulthood."

"Please, I can't tell you."

I squeezed my hands on her wrists a bit more, causing her to wince. I didn't want to hurt her, but I needed her to answer. A female with wolf DNA who was still living was rare. Female wolves were even rarer. Either one would be something one of us would kill to have. Our numbers were dwindling, and it was becoming harder to find a true mate.

I stared hard into her eyes, wondering if she knew how special she was. She had to if she was running away from someone.

I sighed, loosening my grip just a little. "Don't make me repeat my question, Miss Smith. Answer me."

"I don't want you to send me back, please, don't send me back." More tears fell as she sobbed harder.

"I'm going to ask you one more time before I lose my temper with you, Miss Smith," I growled.

I watched as she took in a deep breath and released it.

"I'm from the East Coast. My father is the alpha there. He's a brutal man who's trying to see me married to an even more horrible person than he is. My father didn't care that the one he wants to see me married to beat me badly and tried to rape me before we were wed. My father only wants to breed me. Please, don't send me back." She looked straight into my eyes when she said the last sentence.

My wolf stirred at hearing her story. I wanted to hurt whomever it was that would touch her like that. Her pleas began chipping away the layers of ice that formed around my heart long ago. I released her wrist and tried to soothe her by wiping away her tears.

Realizing that I was making matters worse, I sat up on my knees. I sighed, and then said softly, "Why didn't you tell me?"

"How could I have told you and when would I? You were too busy yelling at me."

I cleared my throat. "I'm sorry for that. Please forgive my brutishness."

"So," she cleared her throat and I could see her eyes glance down at my cock that was still hard and throbbing.

"What do you plan to do with me?" Her eyes met mine and she swallowed.

Her heart was beating hard and I could smell how wet she was, but I could also smell a hint of fear.

"You get some sleep." I heard her sigh as I got up and walked toward her door. She must've been holding her breath, thinking that I was going to harm her like her father had done. "You're safe here with me, but *only* if you stay indoors," I said over my shoulder.

I couldn't look at her, still lying there on her bed, not in the state that I was in. It took all I had to resist going back to her and showing her what I really wanted to do with her. After what she went through, she needed protection from that ever happening again. Me giving in to my wolf and taking her would only cause her to run again, and both my wolf and I wanted her to stay.

I opened the door and closed it calmly before entering my room. Walking into my bathroom, I stopped and stared at myself in the mirror. I took in a deep breath and grumbled. Her scent was all over me. My cock was harder than steel and throbbing so hard it was almost unbearable. My wolf was raging inside me to go back into her room and take her, make her mine. I gripped my length and began stroking it, root to tip. I needed a release.

I stroked harder, trying to bring myself to orgasm, but it wasn't working. It wasn't *my* hand that I wanted stroking me.

Taking in another deep breath, I pulled in her scent again. Shutting my eyes, I could picture her; her sensuous perfect lips closed around the head of my cock, teasing the tip of it with her tongue before she slipped my hardness into her mouth. I tried to picture how it would feel for me to slide farther into her mouth, to touch the back of her throat.

As soon as the images appeared in my mind, my balls pulled up and I was shooting thick ropes of my seed across the vanity and onto the mirror, but I wasn't sated. I wanted more. I wanted *her*.

I wiped up the mess I made and jumped into the shower, turning on the cold water.

It was going to be a long night.

8

Gemma

I woke up to warm sunlight streaming in past the window's sheer curtains. Yawning and stretching away the last remnants of sleep, I remembered where I was. Aiden's estate.

Reluctantly, I had to admit that it was a beautiful place. He was clearly well-off and could care for a pack. Probably could take care of a mate, too.

I shook those thoughts away and stood up, wrapping a sheet around my frame. There weren't any clothes in the bedroom last night, and I was too shaken up after what happened with Aiden to dare leave my room and ask for something cleaner to wear.

But it was morning now, and I couldn't stay in my room forever. I'd done that before and had found the experience rather unseemly. Slowly, I cracked open the bedroom door and strained my ears to listen.

Nothing.

His bedroom door across the hall was open, leading me to believe that he was out. Good. I didn't think I could deal with getting yelled at again. Crossing the room, I picked through the pile of clothes I'd hastily stripped out of last night. In my vest's pocket was the cash Aiden had tucked inside and my phone. I needed to call my supervisor from the catering company and give her a damn good excuse as to why I'd left halfway through my shift.

Pressing the buttons on my phone with increasing aggression, I found it dead. Useless. I cursed and tossed it onto the bed in frustration. My charger was at the motel, and I was forbidden from leaving. How was I supposed to manage without any of my things?

I eyed the uniform, wrinkled from its night on the floor. After a moment's thought, I pulled it on in case Aiden decided to show up.

I was just about to open the bedroom door again to check if the coast was clear when there was a knock. My immediate thought was Aiden, coming to check. I was glad that I hadn't left without permission again.

On the other side was not who I was expecting. Mr. Trenton—John, I mentally corrected—stood in the doorway. He was frowning, but his expression morphed into something like surprise when he saw me.

"You're really here."

I shifted my weight back and forth between my feet, uncertain of what he meant. "Yeah?"

He strode into the bedroom, inviting me to sit on the bed while he took the vanity chair. The way he settled in, it seemed there was a lot to explain. I was mostly confused—how did he know I was here?

"When Aiden told me that you were here, I had to see it for myself."

My eyebrows knitted in confusion.

"I scented you, the day we met." He threw it out casually, like we were discussing what to order for lunch. "I knew you were a wolf from the start ... it didn't seem possible."

Digesting that, I put the pieces together. "So, you're—"

"An omega, yes. Aiden is my brother. Half-brother. We have the same mom."

I nodded and exhaled on a sigh. I honestly didn't think anyone could smell that I was unique. My father never explained that much to me. The cat was already out of the bag now—maybe Aiden hadn't told John about who I really was yet—and I might as well.

"I'm not exactly from this territory … My father is the alpha of the East Coast pack. He was abusive, so I escaped about four months ago and have been on the run ever since." I angled my chin up, trying to look strong to counteract the crying and pleading I'd succumbed to last night with Aiden. "I told your brother last night, and he said I would be safe here."

John nodded immediately. "Damn right. It's a risk to harbor you, especially if your father, an alpha of another pack, is looking for you. But I wouldn't feel right about kicking you out, and I think Aiden shares that sentiment."

His voice had gone soft, showing a gentle compassion I had yet to see from his brother. I supposed that was a prime example of the difference between them. The alpha and the omega. Maybe he could help me make some headway in getting some of my necessities.

"I need my belongings. Phone charger, clothes, stuff like that. I would ask Aiden, but … can you help me?"

"So, you've decided to stay with us?"

I thought about it. The possessive way that Aiden treated me was a clear indicator that he made the decisions around here. Even if I wanted to leave, I didn't think he'd be very happy about it. Especially since he didn't like the looks of the place I was staying at.

"It appears that choice has been made for me." I couldn't hide the bitterness that laced my tone. After spending the entirety of my life under the control of another alpha, I wasn't entirely pleased about having to do it again.

That didn't go unnoticed by John. He sat forward in the chair, propping his elbows on the tops of his thighs. My eyes caught his, dark with concern.

"Did he explain to you what happened? Why he acts the way he does?"

The idea was laughable. Something told me that Aiden was one of those people with a fortress built around his emotions, guarding him from getting hurt. Of course, that meant it was all the more frustrating for me.

"A couple of years ago, he was married." That came as a surprise. Sure, he was attractive, but his temper and demeanor were less than savory. "She was a beautiful, sweet woman. But they were married, not mated. They were actually expecting a baby a few months in. It was a boy."

"What happened?"

"There were complications. See, he never told her that he was a were. He was sure she would turn him away if she knew. And when the complication started, he couldn't do anything but hope that they'd make it and he would tell her later. But there was no way she could survive the birth. She was rushed to the hospital. They had to do an emergency cesarean even though the baby was premature. It was already too late. They couldn't save her, and the baby died soon after."

That was a lot to take in. The way Aiden snapped and was quick to lose his temper made a lot more sense now. I couldn't imagine the pain of losing someone I cared about, especially two people at the same time. The heartbreak that comes with that is something no one should ever have to bear.

What I do remember of my own mother continues to give me nightmares. I made the mistake in sneaking out of my room one night; I must've been five at the time. I heard noises coming from my parent's room that woke me up. I cracked the door open and had seen my father slapping my mother around before forcing himself on her. It was shocking to see what he was doing to her. I ran back to my room, scared and confused. A few days later, my father came into my room to tell me that I would no longer be seeing my mother. That she was gone.

I also couldn't relate to Aiden's previous love. "I guess I'm not the same as her; she was human and, in some aspects, I'm not. That's why my father wants to send me off to another were. He said I could tolerate giving birth because I have werewolf in my DNA."

"You're special, and your father should see that. Our pack desperately needs our alpha to take a mate. His wolf needs it, too. Most of our pack is out running around as wolves, unable to change back because the wolf's presence in our alpha is too strong."

"That must be why he seems so angry all the time," I quipped.

John laughed. "Yes, but some of that is Aiden and not the wolf."

"He didn't tell me any of this."

"He would've. It just would have taken him awhile before he did."

He couldn't really be faulted for that. Still, there was something nagging at the back of my mind. The way he treated me and the things John was telling me ... It just seemed like there was more going on than I was aware of.

"Do you think he truly wants me as his mate?"

"I'm not sure. In the end, it's up to him to see the link between you two and bond with it. Being an omega, I can see it, although faintly. From the moment I met you, I could tell you could be the one for Aiden. For him to see it and admit that it's there, especially after what he went through the last time, would take a lot. It's more likely that he would ignore it for as long as possible. Only he and his wolf will be able to definitively tell whether you're his mate or not. We'll just have to wait and see. Hopefully, it won't be too late when he does come to terms with your connection. Just give him some time. Don't worry, you'll be safe here with us."

I nodded, reeling at the idea of Aiden being my mate. It must have been dumb blind luck that led me to that job a week ago. What were the odds of my mate overseeing the place I would be hired to work for, and on top of that, being the alpha in that territory?

Still, if everything John had said was true, then I'd need to stay here. They offered me protection, in the safety of the pack. The least I could do was cooperate.

I asked John if I could retrieve my belongings from the motel. He agreed, offering to drive. Unlike Aiden, he didn't have a chauffeur and a fancy car—John just had the *other* fancy car. I hadn't seen such luxury when I was at home.

At the motel, John followed me inside. The room was modest: just a bed, dresser, and the door leading to the tiny bathroom. There was an abandoned air to the place. Quickly, I gathered my meager belongings of importance—phone charger, clothes, and the emergency cash I kept stashed in between the pages of an old book I found in the first place I moved into.

John nodded when I finished. "That everything?"

I tried to ignore the bit of surprise in his tone when he saw that I really didn't have much in terms of material possessions. Striding out of the room, I turned down the hallway to get back to the car.

"Gemma … wait a second."

There was apprehension in his voice. Even if I could have sensed it, I didn't need to in order to know that something was wrong. I stopped and turned to look at his face, brows knotted in worry.

My heart rate spiked. "What is it?"

John drew in a breath, scenting the air. I tensed and waited for him to let me know that everything was okay before I moved any farther. I prayed that it was nothing.

He stepped past me and into the hallway, eyes trained to search for movement. There was a thin gush of air that rushed past my ear, and I was helpless to do anything but watch John's knees give out from under him as he collapsed.

A small, red-tipped dart was sticking out of the side of his jugular.

I whirled around to duck back into the room, but a hand reached out and gripped my upper arm. With a noise of protest and fear, I was yanked toward the person who shot John. He held me against the wall by my shoulders.

It was the same man from the night before at the golf club—the one who couldn't leave me alone. There was a sick smirk twisting his face.

"I knew I would have to do things my way. Did you think I was lying when I said I had a job for you?"

"Who are you?" My eyes flickered from his face to John's unconscious form on the ground. I was completely at the mercy of this creepy stranger who had just assaulted my companion.

He laughed cruelly at my ignorance. "It's sad that your dear ol' dad kept you locked up and hidden away from the outside world. You really are so ignorant to our world, aren't you? I'm the second in command to your father and the one your father made the pact with concerning your future offspring."

I frowned up at him, concerned about the lack of knowledge I had about my own father's doings. "I thought I was promised to Mack?"

He grinned. "Yeah, well, Mack disappointed me when he got rough with you the way that he did. Which was possibly my fault."

"Your fault?"

"I told him that if he wasn't man enough to pop your little cherry and get you pregnant already, then I would have to step in and show him how it was done." He shrugged nonchalantly, making me sick to my stomach with his blatant, disgusting disregard for me as a human being. "After all, you do belong to us."

"You're sick if you think I'm going to let either of you near me," I spat in his face, renewing my struggle to free myself from his grip.

He easily slammed me back against the wall, nearly knocking the breath out of me. "Well," he snarled, "you're special, darlin'. There aren't many like you. The pack will be stronger, thanks to you. Just gotta make sure we breed you enough to sire as many wolves as possible." The last words were breathed down my neck, sending an icy, unpleasant shiver through my body. "I am going to enjoy everything I do to you."

He leaned in closely, too closely, and crushed his lips to mine. I tried to move myself off the wall in an attempt to get him off me, but he was more than twice my size. The last thing I registered was the plunge of a needle into the side of my neck.

9

Aiden

It had been too long. Way too long. I knew John was going to take Gemma to the motel—by my request. I had thought she might trust him to accompany her rather than me. A small part of me agreed with that idea.

Except they left six hours ago, and John wasn't responding. The last text he'd sent was a simple "we made it to the motel." He was merely obliging my orders for updates about her whereabouts. What could they possibly be doing still, *for six hours*, at the motel room?

My possessive side offered one unsavory answer to that.

John would never. He was my second, my *brother*. Sure, I'd ignored his suggestions of pursuing something more with Gemma, but that didn't mean *he* was allowed to snatch her up for himself.

I growled out loud at the thought, an echo of the noise resounding through the cavernous living room. My pacing resumed as I yanked my phone from my pocket to check once more. Nothing.

Seven, I decided. Once seven o'clock rolled around, I'd leave for the motel and see what I could find. There had to be some reasonable explanation for this.

I checked my phone again. 6:57. Close enough. I darted to the garage and plucked the keys to my personal car from their hook on the wall. Recalling the address Gemma had told Andrew the night before, I mentally mapped out my route and headed toward the populated, dilapidated side of town.

Once at the motel, I shook my head again in disdain. How could she have been living here for any amount of time? I understood that she didn't have money, but I hadn't known her situation was so incredibly dire.

Glancing around, I took stock of the area around the building. I hadn't gotten her room number, and there wasn't anything to indicate which one they had gone into. It would have to be determined by scent.

Stepping out of the car, ears straining and nose up, I breathed in deeply. John's familiar scent was faint from where I was. I walked closer to the building and caught her intoxicating scent, but with a spike of fear running through it. Something had definitely gone wrong.

The closer I got to the building, the stronger it was. I walked slowly down the open hallway of the motel, sniffing at every door. Her scent was strongest in room twenty-four and dropped off afterward. Doubling back to that one, I tried to distinguish her emotions through the scent.

John's was there too, but fainter. Much fainter. And almost twisted, like something had altered the scent. They weren't inside anymore; that much was certain. So where had they gone?

Out of curiosity, I tested the door. It clicked open easily, unlocked. There was only one reason why they would leave in a hurry without bothering to lock the door.

Sure enough, once inside the room, I smelled it. The same scent of the man from last night's event. The very one I specifically told Gemma to stay away from.

He was here, but why? Was he a part of Gemma's father's pack? Surely, she would have shown some recognition when she had talked to him at the golf club. Maybe her father hired him to find her.

I whipped out my phone, already making mental plans to retrieve them. If John and Gemma were still together, then I could use the location services on John's phone to find them. Glancing around the room, I didn't see the phone anywhere inside. It must still be with them.

The head of security for my pack and estate answered the phone quickly when I called. I filled him in on the situation, letting him know who the man was who had taken them. When I gave him the name and affiliation, he expressed his confidence that he could handle the problem.

Internally, I really hoped so. Not only did he take my brother, but he took Gemma as well. That was unacceptable and a violation against were pack law.

"We're going to get them back," I growled into the phone, "and make him pay. It's possible that John still has his phone on him. Track it and send me the location."

I hung up and stormed back to my car. My heart pounded in my ears. The rage of what had happened caught up with me. *How dare they take her?* I knew I should have protected her better. She shouldn't have ever left my sight, small and weak and human as she was. Especially after learning about her sheltered life. She needed an alpha, someone to protect her. Leaving her with John wasn't acceptable protection.

She needed me.

While sitting in my car and stewing over this, my phone pinged with a text from security. John's phone was in an abandoned warehouse on the other side of town. It was unfamiliar to me but still in my territory. Barely. I quickly called all the members of my pack who were still able to shift between wolf and human form. If there was going to be a fight, I wanted to have my pack on my side.

After starting the car, I quickly drove to the warehouse.

10

Gemma

I blearily opened my eyes, mostly aware of the hard concrete ground under my feet and the pounding in my head. Cringing and groaning, I tried to focus on the room in front of me. It was a large, mostly empty room. Old, water-damaged cardboard boxes were piled along one wall and plastic sheets lined the floor. It had the industrial, tangy smell of a warehouse. My arms ached, and after attempting to move them, I found the rope wrapped around my torso. I was tied, rather annoyingly, to a pole in the center of the room.

Once I caught my bearings, I found John in the mess of the room. He was tied up in coils of thick rope crisscrossing along his naked torso and trailing up to a long metal beam spanning the length of the room. His feet were barely touching the ground, and his chin was tucked to his chest. He hadn't yet woken up from whatever drug we'd been injected with.

Turning, I spotted the man who had taken us. He walked toward us, one hand behind his back and a smirk on his face. A devious satisfaction adorned his face.

"How nice of you to join us again. I hoped you would wake up in time to see the show. We wouldn't want to miss it, now would we?" His voice dripped with glee. He stalked over to John, revealing the whip he'd had hidden behind his back.

My eyes widened in fear as he raised the leather strip above his head. With a sickening crack, it fell upon John's bare skin and raised a red welt. He was still unconscious, so his only reaction was a head loll and an involuntary grunt. I, on the other hand, couldn't help but scream for him to stop. Horror and fear filled my body, making me feel ice cold all over.

The strikes never faltered in their speed or strength, until the whipping finally started to wake John up. His face was contorted with pain. My voice was getting wrecked from screaming for him to stop. "Please! Stop."

"Why?" He whirled around, snarling. "Why do you care for him? Is he the one you were planning on giving yourself to?"

I was too distraught to answer. John didn't deserve to go through this because of me. He was in this position because he was protecting me. Tears streamed down my face while broken sobs escaped my throat.

A high, pained whine emitted from John. His growls weren't the low, threatening variety like alphas were capable of. It was quiet and needy, designed to attract an alpha to protect the omega. Still, even though I wasn't an alpha, the sound broke my heart, and I felt desperate to protect him.

The man dropped the whip onto the ground carelessly in favor of slapping an open palm across John's face. It cracked through the room, echoing, thanks to the emptiness. Who held the dominance in the situation wasn't in question and hadn't been for a while. The strike was purely to wake John up and demonstrate to him who was in control.

He stepped in even closer, getting right in John's face. "So, tell me, are you the mutt that was planning to take my sweet Gemma away from me?"

His claim over me turned my stomach. John didn't answer with words, just an angry growl. His face was still screwed up with pain, but defiance flashed through his eyes. He was holding his own, refusing to give in.

Another slap in the face. "Answer me!" the man screamed, his dominant growl rumbling through the room.

"Leave him alone!" I found my voice again.

Whirling around, he seemed to remember that I was still there. His upper lip curled up in a snarl, and he strode across the room. After looking up and down at my tied-up body, apparently appreciating the view, he tugged the bottom of my shirt up from under the rope. I writhed to try to get away but was helpless to escape his attentions. His hands slid up my stomach and underneath my bra to squeeze at my breasts with an iron-tight grip. I cried out in pain.

His creepy smirk curled up next to my ear. "These are so perfect," he breathed. "I can't wait to see my pups nursing from such luscious tits. I think I should enjoy them first."

I cringed as the man leaned forward to place his mouth on one of my breasts and began to nip and suck on my nipple through my bra. John let out a threatening growl.

"Oh, what's the matter?" He turned exasperatedly to John, his hand creeping below the hemline of my skirt and between my thighs. I clamped my legs closed, trying to prevent his entry into my most intimate spaces. "You don't approve of how I'm handling my woman? I'm planning on breeding her. With her father's alpha blood running through her veins, she'll make a strong brood."

"Please, stop!" I tried begging again, knowing it was useless. "I didn't want to be a part of your contract. This isn't right!"

"You have no choice in the matter. You certainly don't have a say in it either." He growled. "Your father so kindly gifted you to me. Little does he know, once I sire a male child, I plan on taking him out. He's been a fairly useless alpha anyway. The second in command can step up then, and what a happy coincidence that it will be me. I've already been doing most of his job anyway. I'm the rightful alpha. I've taken over many of the small surrounding packs. It won't be long before I take your father's. Most of the pack is already on my side."

His gaze eerily roamed my body and I felt my stomach churn again. "And as for you, you'll continue your life much like you did your childhood, locked in your room. Only difference is, you'll continue giving me more sons and hopefully a daughter or two so I can pass them on to other wolves in my pack."

His words disgusted me, so I spat right in his ugly face. "I hope he kills you."

Unprepared for the strike, I cried out when he backhanded my cheek in retaliation.

"Why don't you let me loose and try that again, but on me," John growled in a low imitation of an alpha. He sounded like he was extending a challenge.

"I knew you'd come around eventually," he turned and, with all the bravado of a man who thought he'd won, strode back toward John. "If she's yours, then why haven't you taken her already?"

"She belongs to my alpha," he sneered in response.

"And where is your alpha, then? I want to show him who she truly belongs to. Mark her and claim her as mine right in front of him."

11

Aiden

I heard the echo of John telling the man about Gemma belonging to his alpha. Something like pride undoubtedly surged through me, even more so when Gemma didn't deny it.

Foster, the man I had told off yesterday, asked smarmily where the alpha was. And wouldn't that just be the perfect time to make my presence known?

"Mr. Foster!" I exclaimed with false cheerfulness, walking in slowly to take in the scene before me. Both

Gemma and John were tied up, in various states of undress. John had been clearly beaten and looked worse for wear. Anger flashed through me at seeing my brother so mistreated. And Gemma with her shirt ripped open. The implications made me sick to my stomach. "I thought I asked you to leave? Politely too, which I must say is rare for someone trespassing on my territory."

"And I told you that you have something that belongs to me. I'm here to collect."

"You didn't tell me that it was a woman." I glanced at her from the corner of my eye. Her face was unreadable, but I could smell the fear and anticipation coming from her. She was terrified, making my instinct to protect her stronger.

"You never asked." He looked so smug, so satisfied with himself, that I wanted nothing more than to wipe that expression right off his face. However, this was going to end, possibly with a fight. I only had one goal: to protect what was mine. Seeing how the two of us were alphas, it seemed there was only one way to resolve this issue.

"You can't take her," I growled.

"Why not?" Foster didn't reciprocate the aggression, trying to prove that he wasn't going to take the bait. I knew it was only a matter of time.

"She's on my territory and she's also mine," I snarled, hating that I had to explain that. My canines lengthened, forcing my mouth open to show my teeth. The wolf in me was practically fighting to show himself, but I restrained the urge to shift just yet.

"I have a written contract that states otherwise. You haven't scent marked her either, meaning she is up for grabs. What were you waiting for anyways?" He taunted, reaching over to grip Gemma's jawline and expose her neck. His nostrils flared when he traced the length of that pretty, pale neck with the tip of his nose. Gemma let out a noise of disgust and squirmed away.

I snarled, trying to warn him against doing so. My wolf was already howling inside, calling out to the other members of the pack. They had arrived on the property, filing in through the various entrances and exits. One of them let out a growl, but I silenced him with a halting hand. If we went through with a challenge, then I had to be the only one in the fight. No sense injuring good men on this filth, and any assistance from another wolf would void the challenge.

"I can't believe she wouldn't have told you about me, or who she is. Do you even know where we come from? Or who her father is?" Foster spat, his anger finally seeping through.

"As a matter of fact, she did. And I stand by what I said. *She's mine.*" I growled and took another step closer to them. John, Gemma and the rest of my pack watched with bated breath to see if Foster would take the words for what they truly were.

"Well now." Foster stepped toward the center of the room, casually. "I guess that's a challenge." He began removing the two-piece suit he was wearing, surely wanting to preserve the expensive piece.

"That it is." I took the opportunity to gain the upper hand as soon as it presented itself.

"Accepted."

Nodding internally to my wolf, I unleashed the beast inside and started shifting. The continuous growl I'd been suppressing turned into a loud snarl as the pain of my body lengthening and stretching took over. The clothes I was wearing were shredded. As soon as I dropped down to all fours, I sprinted toward Foster with intent to kill.

12

Gemma

I could only watch as the two wolves went after each other. Aiden seemed much more intimidating, shifting into his wolf form so quickly. He sounded furious, barely concealing it when he and the man—Mr. Foster, I mentally corrected—were talking.

"She's mine."

I couldn't deny the affect those words had on me. My eyes had gone wide when he'd growled it so possessively. Something in me stirred every time he insisted upon it.

Arousal, yes, but also a deep desire to go to him. I wanted to be with him, to let him claim me and keep me safe. I trusted him to be my mate a lot more than these other assholes.

My gut instinct told me I was right to choose Aiden over my father's second. A shiver ran through me when he told me who he was. I had no idea. Maybe I *was* too sheltered, as I didn't know who Mr. Foster was until he told me. What I did know was that I didn't want to go with him.

The fight before me was horrific. The two wolves—one a chestnut brown and the other a dull gray streaked with black—lunged toward each other, aiming for the neck each time. Aiden used his teeth to rip out pieces of flesh from the other wolf, and his paws to pin him down.

Foster used his hind legs to regain the upper hand, and the two rolled across the cement floor. The sounds were vicious, reverberating through the wide space. Everyone in the room was completely focused on the fight, and out of respect for the significance of the challenge, no one interfered.

Foster let out a long, high howl of pain. Aiden had regained control of the fight and quickly clamped his jaws onto the other wolf's neck. Slick, red blood coated both their furs, and gleamed over the white of Aiden's teeth. My jaw dropped at the implications of such a lethal final blow. A pool of red began collecting across the cement floor.

The gray wolf's body went gradually limp, as Aiden's grip on his neck never faltered. The pool of blood grew far too large for hope of recovery.

Aiden let out a low growl, unclamping his jaws as the challenge had been won.

He limped away, still in his wolf form. There were long scratches and bites along his front legs and torso, bleeding sluggishly. Aiden's wolf moved with his tail held high and head lowered threateningly as he limped out of the room.

One of the other weres from the pack moved to release John from his restraints, taking several moments to get his clothes back on. His injuries made that much more difficult and delicate. The other weres looked at me warily, like they were afraid to touch me. I supposed that made sense, given the challenge had been won by their alpha.

Aiden limped back in, dressed in a button-down and slacks. He must have gotten a change of clothes from his car, I realized. There were still scratches and cuts bleeding through the fabric. He immediately sought me out, yanking on the rope holding me to the pole. His touch was hardly gentle, almost angry. Our eyes found each other, mine no doubt fearful and his hard with irritation. He glared at the bruise on my face from when Foster had slapped me, letting out an angry growl.

He took off his shirt and wrapped it around me, after taking in how ripped and ruined my own was. His eyebrows were knotted together in anger and worry. John approached carefully, murmuring in a low, soothing tone to Aiden that he was going to head back to the house.

"C'mon," he forced out wearily. "Let's get back too."

His hand reached out for mine even though I didn't need any help. Would it be weird to take it? I didn't think so, given the claim he'd apparently staked over me. It wouldn't be wise to say no, but I didn't want to. After taking his hand, I considered what the current state of our relationship was supposed to be now. Did I belong to him? Had my allegiance simply shifted from one alpha to another without any say on my part?

Was Aiden accepting the bond that was between us, as John had said?

I didn't know. Aiden's grip on my hand was tight—not like a gentle lover but more like a child scared of losing their favorite toy. Maybe I really was like a doll to him, just something to have, meant to entertain him and show off to his pack. It was obvious they knew I was his.

But that couldn't be the case. If there was a bond between us, wouldn't that influence the way he treated me? I didn't have positive experiences with alphas. They were supposed to be possessive, yes, but also incredibly caring and gentle with the ones they truly loved.

I would just have to wait to see how he decided to treat me.

13

Aiden

I strode up to the house, tugging Gemma along by the hand. Those of my pack who had stayed behind had waited near the front door for news of what had happened, but I had to ignore them for now. There was too much to unveil, too much to deal with on the front of whatever had just happened.

We went upstairs to the bedroom, immediately. I didn't even think of the implications of that, or what Gemma might think, but given the fact that I had just won a challenge over the right to mate with her, it could mean something I didn't intend. Thinking quickly, I went into the bathroom to check my wounds. They would provide a good enough distraction.

They throbbed dully with pain, but it wasn't anything that I couldn't ignore. I had been ignoring it for the whole ride back. Several long scratches and bite marks were along my rib cage and upper back, but the blood was already drying and scabbing over.

Gemma appeared in the doorway, shyly peeking around the corner. My state of undress seemed to distract her, or make her a little shy. It was almost amusing, how sweet and innocent she truly was. I grabbed a bottle of hydrogen peroxide from underneath the cabinet and the box of tissues from the counter, preparing to treat my wounds. She stepped in fully, holding out her hands in a silent command.

After I handed over the disinfecting supplies, she set to work cleaning the wounds. Each tissue got slowly bloodier, and some more than others. The process of cleaning them stung, making me wince. For a while, we were both silent. She was concentrating entirely on the task and I on her.

There was a captivating quality to her, with those brown doe eyes and the rosy red curve of her lips. Even with her brow knotted in focus and her bottom lip tucked between her teeth, I found myself appreciating that uncommon beauty.

Gemma opened her mouth several times, like she was about to say something. Eventually, I sighed and murmured in what I hoped was a gentle tone. "Spit it out."

"What are you planning on doing now?" she asked quietly.

I mulled over the possibilities in my head. The challenge meant that I could do whatever I pleased with her, but I would never do something without her approval or permission. And when word got back to her father of the loss of not only his daughter but also his second in command … it would undoubtedly get ugly. Best to get ahead of it, to extend some kind of olive branch.

"I will need to call your father and tell him what happened. If he doesn't hear the news from me personally, there could be problems," I explained as softly as I could, so as not to scare her. I wanted her to know that I was on her side and I was going to protect her.

She paused wiping away the disinfectant to look at me with wide eyes. She took a deep breath in, almost like a soft sigh, and then she continued running the tissues over the long wounds in my skin.

"Some of these are really deep." I could tell she was forcing herself to sound casual, but her concern seeped through, and her scent betrayed her.

"They will heal with time." I watched her lips form a pout.

Her eyes on my face forced my own upward. "You could've died. He was determined to kill you and anyone else in his way to make sure I was his."

"That didn't happen." I reached out carefully, running gentle fingertips along her bare arm. "Look, if this isn't what you want, you need to tell me. I don't want you to think that I'm keeping you captive here."

She sighed, pausing. I could practically hear the wheels turning as she weighed her options. "Honestly ... I want my freedom. That's why I left in the first place, that's how I ended up here in your territory. I can never go back to my father, and the life he wanted for me."

"As long as you're in my territory, you'll be safe," I stated firmly. No doubt could be left in her mind that she was taken care of here. "I will protect you and so will my pack. Even if you choose not to stay here in this house."

Those eyes held my gaze once more, growing more intense with each passing second. "I think ... I'm not quite ready to leave just yet. Not until ... until all of this is behind us."

Us. I kind of liked that.

"You're welcome to stay here as long as you need to."

"I would like that." She nodded, looking distressed.

A lone tear escaped, finally. It wasn't the first time I'd seen her cry or show her vulnerability. The fact that someone out there was making her feel this way made my blood boil and made the need to protect her surge up inside of me. Still, I was glad she seemed to trust me enough to show her true emotions. I wiped away the tear with my thumb but didn't pull away. My hand cupped her face, and she thankfully leaned into the touch. That bottom lip, bitten red, was pulled between her teeth once more.

The desire to pull her into my arms and taste her grew far too great. Didn't she know how tempting she was, how crazy her scent drove me? I could only hope that something about me made her feel a fraction of the same insanity I experienced. My wolf loved that scent and craved it when she wasn't around. Last night, I'd gotten a taste and couldn't seem to forget it.

She glanced up into my eyes, and I knew I had to do something. The distance between us was so unbearable—so I darted forward, too quickly to stop myself. My hands wrapped around her waist, yanking her body to press against my own. Moving slowly was out of my control; the wolf was animalistic and desperate to get her lips on mine.

Our lips crashed more than met. She moaned, a sweet sound that forced a wave of heat to flood my abdomen and all of my blood to rush even further south. After the day we'd had, I felt nothing but relief at tasting her lips. Hell, I hadn't kissed anyone like this in so long that I felt all the tension built up over the years dissipate. She did this to me; she made me feel finally at ease and comfortable.

Like a bonded mate should.

That thought terrified me beyond anything else. I knew she wasn't malicious, but the possibility of her having that much power over me was too much to deal with.

I ended the kiss as quickly as I could without hurting her. She appeared surprised, but I just couldn't explain … not yet.

So, I ran away. For good measure, I slammed the front door closed to ensure she didn't follow.

14

Gemma

The door slamming made me jump a little. I wasn't scared, just worried. His face after our kiss was troubled, almost terrified. I hadn't even seen that look when he was fighting Mr. Foster during the challenge. Did kissing me really scare him that much?

I was conflicted. Aiden seemed like such a hard ass, frankly rude, controlling alpha male when I had first met him—but it was clear that he was so much more than that. He has been hurt; that much was clear. There were walls built up around him, preventing him from letting me in. The question was, should I stay and see if the attraction we had was real? Or leave now and cut my losses before I got hurt myself?

It'd be a lot easier to decide if he was just a hard ass, rude, controlling alpha male.

I had said that I wanted to stay. My gut kept telling me it was the right decision even though my head wasn't entirely sold. Maybe I was overthinking everything; if I based the decision on the kiss we had just shared, it would be easy. I craved more of him, and the way he just took what he wanted. Something deep inside of me craved it too and wished he would give me everything we both wanted instead of running away.

Shaking my head, I stepped out of Aiden's bedroom and went across the hall to my own. After the day I'd had, I felt the need for a long shower. Anything to wash away the gross feeling of Mr. Foster's hands on me.

There were toiletries—thankfully unused and clean—ready to use in their various places around the bathroom. Eagerly, I hopped in the shower and allowed the steam to wash over me.

The heat around me reminded me of the heat of a different kind pooling between my legs. The kiss with Aiden was so incredible—and nothing like I'd imagined my first kiss with him to be. His hands were all over me, taking and grabbing at what he knew was rightfully his. I tried to mimic that, running my own hands over my waist and stomach like he had. It wasn't the same, but I had enough of an imagination to keep going.

If he hadn't ended the kiss, what would have happened? My hand drifted down lower, lower than he had gone. I imagined it was his fingertip rubbing over my clit. Fueled by the memory of his lips and hands on me, slick quickly coated my fingers, making the glide easier. I lifted one foot up to the edge of the tub, spreading my legs to better access myself.

If Aiden was here, would he drop to his knees and put his mouth on me? How would his tongue feel where my finger was, flicking and running along the bud of my clit? Would he be a tease, or ruthless with the pleasure he provided? How long would he spend licking me before he decided to cut to the chase and claim me?

I moaned, throwing my head back. I didn't know where the thought came from, but it excited me even farther. The pleasure settled low in my gut, tightening and coiling. My inexpert fingers worked more off instinct than anything—I hadn't touched myself enough in my life to really know what I was doing. This time was better, thanks to the ideas that kiss had put in my head.

The harder I stroked my swollen bud and the deeper into the fantasy I fell, the tighter that coil of arousal became inside of me. I wanted Aiden so badly. Getting just one taste of how he felt pressed against me wasn't nearly enough. I needed more.

I needed him to claim me for his own.

I shuddered as the pleasure peaked. The orgasm crashed through my body in waves, forcing a long moan from me. My muscles clenched, and I gasped with the force of it. Finally, my clit grew too sensitive to keep rubbing it, and I had to cease.

Catching my breath, I tried to recover. Afterward, I felt wonderfully relieved and almost floaty. It was like the tension that had been building since I'd arrived here was finally expelled. I quickly finished the shower and collapsed into bed. Even falling asleep was easier, though the dreams weren't exactly pleasant.

The gray wolf clamped its jaws around the neck of the other, blood spattering sickly across the concrete floor. It landed on my face, hot and red and obscuring my vision.

The wolf shifted back into a man with a sick grin and snarl.

I was back in my childhood bedroom, too familiar for comfort. The man was dragging me in by a firm grip on my arm. Looking down, I saw my nakedness and quickly went to cover myself with my hands. He laughed and threw me onto the twin bed I'd grown up sleeping in.

He forced my legs open and entered me roughly, wrenching a scream from my throat. Suddenly, I had replaced myself with my mother and instead of it being my father, it was Mr. Foster.

A knock on my bedroom door woke me from the nightmare. Several seconds passed as I struggled to catch my breath and lower my heart rate.

Groggily, I managed to get out of bed and opened the door, surprised to see Aiden on the other side. He had left in such a stormy way last night I figured he would be gone for a lot longer. Still, he looked at me with worry in his eyes and took in my barely awake appearance.

"I spoke to your father." He cut right to the chase. "He's not happy to hear that you've chosen to stay here and that his second in command is dead."

I shook my head, trying to clear some of the sleep from it and wrap my head around this. That was where Aiden had gone last night? Had he seen my father in person? He couldn't have; there was too much space between the territory I was running from and the one I was currently in. It must have been over the phone.

"Can't say I'm surprised. Did you tell him that the same second was planning on killing him and taking over his reign as alpha?"

"No." Aiden stepped in, dropping heavily onto the vanity chair. He looked absolutely exhausted. "Didn't think there was any point. If there are more of his people planning a coup, that might actually work in our favor. It's best for him to think everyone on his side is actually on his side. He did say that he wants you to come back, and he threatened to come here and take you himself. I think he's planning on another challenge."

He leaned back in the chair, running his hands over his face. That was the last thing he needed, seeing as he was still healing from the previous day's challenge. Two in a row might actually kill him, even if he did win. Was I really worth all this?

"What did you say?" I frowned and wrapped one of the bedsheets around myself.

"That if he doesn't at least try to resolve this peacefully, he will end up like his second in command."

The implications of that didn't need to be verbalized. My father would be dead if he didn't cooperate. But would Aiden have enough strength to take up the challenge?

"He said you have one week to return home. After that, he's going to find you."

One week. I supposed that wasn't too soon … maybe we could figure something out before then. We had to— well, I had to. I couldn't be on the run for the rest of my life.

And I certainly couldn't rely on Aiden for the rest of my life either; he had already given me so much. I couldn't put him and his pack in any more danger.

"I'm sorry. I know this is a lot for you, and it's all in the name of keeping me safe, so … thank you. And I'm sorry."

His lips quirked up in a soft smile, like I was a silly child he was fond of. It was a little condescending but probably justified. I was genuinely grateful but also really trying to cover my bases and not piss him off.

"Don't worry. This is just how were politics works. I need to keep you safe, and I'll do whatever it takes to make sure that happens." He paused, taking in a deep breath. "In fact, there is another option that we could employ to force your father to stand down. Something that would relinquish any claim he has over you."

I perked up at that, ready for any suggestions he had.

"What is it?"

15

Aiden

I had every right to claim her. My wolf knew this and was shouting at me to do so. *Sorry, bud, if I did it your way, she probably wouldn't have anything to do with me afterward.* It would've been urgent and rough, and she needed the complete opposite. I came close to taking her last night, right there in the bathroom.

It took every ounce of strength I had left to walk out of that room, leaving her in one piece. It angered my wolf when I refused him what was his—ours. I needed to calm him—

both of us—down enough to reason with him. There was only one way we could have her without her running away scared and to protect her from her father or anyone else from taking her against her will.

"Marry me."

Her eyes grew impossibly wide at my proclamation. I knew it was crazy, insane, too soon. We had only kissed once, but there was increasing need and attraction there. Being around her in my wolf form had left me so aroused and desperate that I had masturbated like a horny teenager. I had realized after the fact that once my wolf had scented her that she was a possible mate for me. Still, if we weren't under the current circumstances, there would be no way I would be rushing this.

Yet, it was necessary. If we were married, her father would have no choice but to stand down. For another alpha to come onto my territory, take my mate, and leave with her would be a direct challenge. The community didn't tolerate that violation, and the offending alpha would be put to death.

Either way, if Gemma and I were wed, her father wouldn't be an issue anymore. Plus, I, *we,* needed her.

"Look." Her silence made me nervous, so I launched into an explanation. "I know that when we first met … I was hostile towards you. I'm sorry for that, but I only reacted that way due to your scent. My wolf is drawn to you, and I think you could be my mate." I stared at my hands, twisting them around. "When I shifted and I smelled you … I knew it. I can't deny it anymore, not when we have a solution to our problem right in front of us. This entire time, my instincts have been telling me to claim you, to bond with you, to make you mine. But it's ultimately your choice. So, I'll continue fighting that urge until you give me your decision. I can at least give you that."

I couldn't imagine why, but tears began to well up in her eyes. Was she truly that unused to being treated with kindness and basic decency? My wolf whined at the sight and I wanted to wrap my arms around her, but I didn't budge from my seat.

"Thank you," she mumbled quietly and with finality. I knew she didn't have an answer ready for me just yet. That was okay. We had a week before the situation became dire.

I nodded and stood to take my leave. "Take your time. I'll give you some space in the meantime, okay?"

She nodded and kept staring at the floor, a blush tinting her cheeks. It took a lot of willpower to leave that bedroom and leave her behind. My wolf whimpered at me to go to her, wrap my arms around her, and tell her everything would be all right. But he stepped back, seeing that I was giving my mate what she needed.

My mate.

I smiled at those words. I only hoped she could see it.

16

Gemma

Rendered entirely speechless, I could only sit in shock on the bed. Aiden had just *proposed*. Of course, it wasn't much of a traditional proposal, but still. In essence, that was what had just happened.

It was such a surprise to me that I couldn't even bring myself to answer him. In my head, I knew the answer was yes. My heart wasn't nearly ready, but there was an attraction there. Was it possible for us to be bonded mates? Would I regret signing away my availability to any other man with this marriage?

It was a risk, for sure. But, considering my father was threatening a full-on pack war if we didn't cooperate, the benefits would far outweigh the risks.

I appreciated how he let me make the decision separate from him. Even though I knew my answer pretty much immediately, there was no way I could form the words in any sort of eloquent way. Hell, even several minutes removed from the situation, I was still in shock.

He asked to marry me.

He had acknowledged the possibility of us being mates! I definitely hadn't expected that either. His words resonated with me.

"My instincts have been telling me to claim you, to bond with you, to make you mine."

I wanted him to do just that so much.

I made the decision right then and there to give him my answer later that night. It was enough time to consider my options, but not so much that he'd be worried. Dinner, I decided.

Lazing around all day was torturous. I started planning the dinner, preparing to have it ready by seven. I figured chicken would be a safe bet. Steak seemed like it'd be more appropriate, but I had no idea how he preferred it.

Once everything was cooked and ready, I placed it on the table. I didn't know where he'd gone after speaking with me that morning, but I assumed he was with his pack or in the house. He'd have to come and eat eventually, right?

Half an hour passed. I put the chicken in the oven, to keep it warm and relatively fresh. I could just take it out when he arrived.

Except he didn't arrive.

How was I supposed to give him my answer if he wasn't going to show?

Two hours passed. I'd found a novel to read in Aiden's office to entertain myself until he showed up.

At ten o'clock, I decided he wasn't going to come home and the food was too cold anyway. I still took the chicken out of the oven and arranged it on the table just so he would see what he had missed when he came back.

I wearily got dressed for bed and tried to put my disappointment out of my mind.

My sleep wasn't uninterrupted. Another nightmare plagued me, seemingly for hours.

"Open your mouth."

My father's voice commanded, forcing a sob from my throat. The nightmare was the same as last night with Aiden's wolf dead next to me. Tears streamed down my face as I saw the blood pooling around him. This time, my father was standing in my room, watching Mr. Foster as he pawed at me.

I stared at my father, shaking my head in defiance. It was the same thing he said to my mother that night many years ago.

I watched my father's eyes change from a light brown to a dull amber. He snarled, showing his canines as they begin to lengthen. He was on the verge of shifting and I was being disobedient.

"I said, open your mouth," he growled. Hesitantly, I complied.

Mr. Foster's prick passed my lips, making him practically purr with satisfaction.

"You know what'll happen if you bite," Mr. Foster warned.

I did know. I wasn't sure exactly how I knew, but I did.

I screamed, but it was muffled around the length in my mouth. He placed his hands behind my head, curling his fingers in my long locks, and shoved himself farther into my mouth, causing me to gag as I felt him touch the back of my throat.

"That's right, girl, choke on my cock," Mr. Foster growled.

He thrust his dick in and out of my mouth until I felt bile rush up into my mouth.

"You better not spit that out," Mr. Foster warned. "Here, let me help you."

I had time to take in a deep breath before Mr. Foster shoved his dick in as far as he could, slipping himself down my throat. I started to pull back, but his fingers had a painfully tight grip on my hair.

"Swallow my cock, girl. Take it!"

"You better listen to your mate," my father warned.

I was choking for air now. Mr. Foster wasn't going to budge. I looked over at Aiden, my actual mate, but my tears were obscuring my view. All I could see was a blur lying on the floor. Desperately, I wished Aiden would get up even though I knew he was dead and there was nothing he could do to save me from my fate.

I could hear him, though. Somehow, he was calling out to me.

"Gemma! Wake up, you're okay."

I strained to listen to his voice over the gagging noises I was making.

"Come on, Gemma, come back to me."

I shut my eyes and pictured Aiden's handsome face. His gentle touch. His passionate kisses.

Slowly, the nightmarish scene with Mr. Foster and my father disappeared, turning into darkness before my eyes. I could vaguely hear Aiden's voice once more, guiding me back to sleep. The warmth of the bed and the solid feeling of Aiden holding me made me feel safe once more.

Morning came, punctuating my sleep with the sunlight streaming through the windows. I groaned and stretched, letting my feet creep along the length of the bed. They brushed against—fur?

I sat up quickly, eyes already wide. There was a chocolate-brown wolf lying at the foot of the bed, curled up, with its eyes half-opened with sleep. He whimpered, a soft gentle noise. Nonaggressive.

"Aiden?"

He repeated the noise, hopped off the bed, and trotted out of the bedroom—I assumed to go to his own. I checked my phone while he did, and when he returned, he was in his human form. Thankfully clothed.

Tentatively, he moved to sit at the edge of the bed. When I didn't reject him, he sat next to me.

"Morning." He offered a small smile. "I didn't want to frighten you if you woke up with me lying in bed with you in my human form."

That was actually pretty considerate of him. I nodded and smiled back.

"Thank you." I figured it wouldn't be so bad to wake up next to him in the morning. "I just wasn't expecting you after..."

After he had completely left the premises after dropping the huge bomb of a marriage proposal.

The mood must have shifted in the room or Aiden was a mind reader because he immediately launched into an apology. "I'm sorry for leaving so soon ... I just didn't expect you to be ready with an answer so soon. And when you didn't reply—not that I'm saying you were wrong in doing so—but I just wasn't sure if I should have asked you to marry me or not. I decided to go for a run, distract myself."

That sounded ... reasonable. Crap. Now I looked like the crazy worried wife who expected her husband to always be at her beck and call. I beamed at the thought of being his wife.

"Well, I'm sorry too. For not answering you even when I knew the answer immediately. I was just taken by surprise, you know? But I did think about it some more and I wanted to tell you over dinner."

"And I screwed that up. Listen." He sighed, running his fingers through his hair. "It wasn't exactly easy for me to ask you—"

"Yeah," I interrupted to save him the trouble of rehashing something so personal to him. "John already filled me in about what happened to your wife and child."

He looked surprised, eyebrows lifting and then knotting together. A little grunt of displeasure escaped him.

"Did he now?"

I regretted opening my big mouth. "I hope he's not in trouble for telling me about that."

Aiden sighed, shifted a little uncomfortably. "No … actually, I'm kind of glad that he did. It's just difficult for me to talk about. I would have told you, eventually, but I was unsure of when or how to do it. But I think after I've asked you to marry me, I might be obligated to fill you in."

I appreciated that sentiment and was definitely glad he didn't wait until after we were married to tell me he had already had a family. But I still had underlying insecurities.

"I hope you weren't uncomfortable with me being in your bed when you woke up. You were screaming out in your sleep and I rushed in here to see that you were having a bad dream."

"I'm not uncomfortable with it. And, yes, I have them from time to time."

"Listen, I'm not letting that happen to you again. I am always going to be there for you, no matter what."

"If you're having second thoughts about asking me to marry you—"

"I'm not." He rushed to answer, stating it firmly. "However, if you decide that you need more time to think on it, I understand."

I took in a deep breath, letting it out shakily. "My answer is yes."

17

Aiden

I turned to look at Gemma, mouth slightly agape. Sure, I had asked her to marry me, but I wasn't completely confident that she'd say yes.

But she did.

And she was staring at me with a small smile and nervous eyes.

I didn't have to hold back so much anymore. Instinct could finally win out, at least to a degree.

I leaned in quickly, reaching a hand up to cup her cheek. My heart was pounding with how desperate the need to kiss her unashamedly was after all of this buildup. We both fell back onto the bed after our lips met, me on top of her. Her hands crept over my waist carefully, like she wasn't sure where she was allowed to touch. As I kissed her, I grabbed her hips and the round curve of her bottom, showing her that it was okay.

She moaned against my lips, opening her legs to allow me to settle in between them. Blood was already rushing south, just from having her so close. We moved together, eagerly pressing our bodies against each other.

My phone rang loudly, but my mind was so clouded by the woman under me I could barely even hear it. She jumped though, breaking the kiss off. Undeterred, I kept going, leaning down to drop kisses on her neck. I traced my tongue over her sensitive flesh right between her neck and shoulder and felt the urgent need to mark her, but her voice snapped me out of my daze.

"Don't you need to see if that's someone important?" She threw her head back. I hummed and gently nipped at her neck.

"You're probably right ... but I doubt that it is." Reaching into my pocket, I whipped out my phone to check the caller ID.

It was the same number I had called for an audience with one of the eastern territory's alphas. Gemma's father.

Arousal quickly fading, I frowned and practically ran from the room. I only paused to murmur a reassurance to Gemma and picked up the call.

"Hello?"

"Mr. McKinney. So glad I could catch you." He sounded incredibly cheerful, a definite shift from our last conversation. "I just wanted to let you know that I am in town, and was hoping we could get an opportunity to meet up and chat? You know, alpha to alpha."

My frown deepened. *'Alpha to alpha?'* Like we were gangsters in rival mobs. Still, I was worried. There was no way he could know about the plan for Gemma and me to get married, not yet anyway. I had hoped she and I had enough time, but it seemed as if Gemma's father was an impatient alpha. He wasn't going to wait a week. He was going to come get her now.

"Okay … I have several offices available on my estate. You're welcome to come here." Allowing him onto my turf would keep him on edge since he would be in foreign territory.

"I think I will. I look forward to meeting you in person." He hung up without letting me get the last word in.

Once the line was free, I dialed John and let him know about our new guest. I told him to keep his eyes open and the rest of the pack nearby, just in case.

And then there was just one person left to tell.

"Sorry about that." I returned to the bedroom but didn't enter fully. Once I did, it might be too difficult to leave again.

"It's okay." She smiled from the bed, looking relaxed and sated. "Important alpha business?"

"Something like that." I sighed. "That was your father. He's here."

She sat up quickly, eyes widening with fear. "Is he going to take me?"

"No. I hate to ask this of you, but you need to stay in your room until I tell you it's safe for you to come out." Displeasure wafted through her scent. "I know, but it's how I can keep you safe until he leaves. You understand?"

Gemma nodded, hugging her knees to her chest. It was such a defensive gesture that I had to reassure her more strongly. I crossed the room and pulled her into a long kiss, only ending it once her scent had lost the tinge of fear to it.

John was waiting for me in my office, accompanied by a tall man with salt and pepper hair. His face was twisted up in a strange imitation of a smile.

"Thank you, John. That will be all." I dismissed the omega. He nodded once and left immediately, not wanting to get caught in a standoff. I knew he'd stay close by should I need him.

"So." I rounded the desk, shifting around a few out of place items on the top. His eyes tracked my movement. I sat in the chair and settled in. "What can I help you with?"

He remained standing and sighed, like he was severely put-upon. "Well, I couldn't wait a week. I have come here to take Gemma home with me, where she belongs." He grinned widely again. "I feel we can overlook any trouble she may have caused you."

"Trouble? Gemma is nothing of the sort," I said, pasting on a fake smile.

"Oh?"

"In fact, she and I are engaged to be married," I said, smiling. My canines were itching to lengthen to show him my indifference toward him showing up here. There was no way he was taking her with him. She was staying right here, with me.

"Well, I guess I should offer my congratulations then."

That was surprising. It was also a blatant lie. I was sure whatever he actually wanted to do was far more malicious.

"Is that all you wanted to tell me?"

He smirked, tracing his fingertip over a glass paperweight sitting on the desk. "Of course. We are both reasonable men, good leaders. Why would I ruin relations between our territories with silliness and pettiness?"

Without pause, he grabbed the paperweight and lifted it quickly over his head. I dodged, but not quick enough. The first hit landed directly on my temple, and I was barely aware of a second and third strike before I lost consciousness.

18

Gemma

I heard a loud bang on the bedroom door. Scrambling, I started to run toward the window. Hiding would be useless; my father would just be able to scent me and find me. I stared at the window, remembering how high up I was. It would be a bad landing, but a broken leg or two would be better than leaving here with my father. With a second bang on the door, it swung open.

I heard rather than saw my father enter, storming in like he owned the place. My mind went blank with fear as I darted for the window. He was already growling in anger. His canines lengthened and his eyes darkened as he was on the verge of shifting.

"Had I known you would drive off, I would have never allowed that so-called tutor to teach you how to drive. I took care of her though. Did you really think I'd let you get away, just like that?" His hand clamped on my arm, yanking me back toward him.

I shrieked and tried to wrench myself away. Where was Aiden? All of the possibilities flashed through my mind.

"What did you do to Aiden?!"

My father snarled. "I took care of him, which was something my second was apparently incapable of doing."

I was dragged out of the room, with one of his hands on my arm and the other in my hair, yanking it painfully. Weakly, I focused enough to smack him a few times, but it wasn't nearly enough to free myself. Not only was my father almost twice my size, he was far more powerful than me, so I'd have to rely on other methods to break him down.

"Your so-called second was planning on taking over the pack. After he claimed me, he was going to kill you!"

This didn't seem to surprise him. He kept walking through the various hallways of the large estate, dragging me along.

"Doesn't matter. He's dead now, and I have another contract lined up. The northeastern alpha is expecting you, and since no one else is competent enough to extract you, I've been forced to do it myself."

"You can't take me! Aiden asked me to marry him and I said yes. He'll fight for me." We paused our journey though the estate for a moment while he smirked smugly.

"Well, we don't have to worry about him. He's been dealt with."

The implication of that was almost too much to deal with. Had he murdered Aiden in cold blood? Was my father really capable of that? My breath hitched, but I couldn't let my father know just how much that bothered me.

"I'll just run away again. I'll disappear, like I did last time. I know how, and I know where I made my mistake with the last time." I tipped my chin up in defiance and false confidence.

His fingers wrapped tightly around my arms, and his claws dug into my skin even more as he pushed me into the wall. I made a noise of protest, and he got even closer to my face, sneering. "Listen to me very carefully. You are *mine*, Gemma. You belong to me. You're going to do as I say, and then, once I deliver you to your new alpha, you'll do as he says. Since we've had problems with you willingly allowing any male to fuck you, I'm going to have to watch and make sure this one claims you and makes you his. He's already aware of the fact that he's going to have to keep you in line and keep you locked up."

Struck with horror and fear of my nightmares coming true, I opened my mouth to retort. I never got a chance to, for something dark and quick flashed right by me. There was a low snarl, which in combination with the thing darting right into my line of vision, made me nearly jump out of my skin. It was a wolf upon closer inspection, and it knocked both my father and I to the ground.

I scrabbled away on all fours, eyes wide and gasping. The wolf began tearing into the mass on the floor that was my father. I couldn't bear to watch, so I backed into one of the adjacent hallways and waited for the screams to stop. The sounds were so horrific—snarling and flesh ripping and anguished cries.

After a few more seconds, the noises ceased. There was a small wolfish whimper and then a human groan. Aiden slowly approached around the corner separating the hallways. He was naked, having just shifted back into his human form, but I couldn't even be bothered by that at the moment. My father had just tried to kidnap me, claimed Aiden was dead, and then died a few feet away from me.

Aiden dropped to the floor with me, pulling me into his arms. "You are *mine*, not his or any other."

I let out a shuddering sob and melted into his embrace, finally feeling safe. He had saved me, yet again.

"I thought you were—" I couldn't even bring myself to say the word.

Aiden looked down at me, smiling. "I'm much tougher than he thought I was. And I have someone to look after now. It's not my time yet."

I ran my hands through his dark locks and felt a sticky dampness cover my fingers. "You're wounded."

"I'll heal. Are you … did he hurt you?"

The gentleness in his voice made me smile. "No. I'm okay now."

His lips crushed to mine, and all I could think about was him and how I couldn't live without him.

19

Aiden

I decided right then and there, even though the main threat was gone, I still had to marry Gemma. There was still an alpha waiting for his new mate in the northeast territory that might come sniffing around once he hadn't received his end of the negotiation.

That was a pretty compelling reason, but besides that, I also wanted to.

I didn't need to tell her that for her to know. It was sort of just assumed that we would still be engaged after the death of her father. The only difference between then and now was that we had plenty of time to plan a real wedding and have a true marriage. There was no rush anymore.

So, we moved at our own pace. We went on with our business and started our relationship from the beginning, the way it should have been from the start. I worked to keep the peace between our territory and those surrounding us but also to expand the territory itself. If our pack could be strengthened by the bond between Gemma and I, then we needed to take advantage of that.

And that bond wasn't just beneficial for my pack, either. Finally, I had someone I could trust again. Someone I could be truly intimate with and develop an emotional connection to. After what had happened with my last wife, I wasn't sure I'd ever find that again.

I was sorely mistaken.

Gemma was so sweet, so innocent. Not naïve or ignorant, but genuinely full of wonder and amazement at all the things we would do. It took a lot of effort, but I restrained myself enough to not move too quickly. I was taking everything slow with her. There was just something about her that drove me wild and made me hungry to claim her as my own. That got better over time, of course, the more I scent marked her. But nothing would be quite as permanent as a bonding mark.

One night, I'd had enough of her pale neck going unmarked. As I lay underneath her and allowed her to climb on top of me, I eyed the smooth skin of her neck. To an alpha, it was like looking at a blank canvas, just waiting for an artist to leave his unique painting. I leaned up and kissed right over the point I wanted to leave my mark.

Her legs were bracketing my own, bare except for the silk of her panties. I'd already removed our clothes except for the thin materials of our underwear. My cock was plumping up in my shorts.

Trailing my nose lightly over the column of her neck, I groaned. "I want to bond with you."

She slid over to my right, keeping her body pressed close but dismounting me. There was a look in her eyes, like she wanted something more than what we were doing at the moment. I was more than familiar with that craving but had been holding back for her.

"Why don't you?" she asked teasingly. My hands ran over the curve of her thigh, up over her bottom, and to the dip in her spine. Her bare breasts pressed against my chest, and then her lips were ghosting right over mine. "What's stopping you?"

Her voice was low, that husky whisper saved for lovers. The game she was playing was dangerous, turning me on easily.

"Didn't know if …" I began as she started kissing my neck messily, distracting me as I tried to speak. "If you were ready for that."

"Why would you even have to wonder?" Her hand trailed over my chest, down over my stomach, and under the waistband of my shorts. Thin fingers curled tentatively around my length. My wolf was more than ready to go, wanting to knot her and tie us together.

My hips twitched upward in interest. "You want me?"

She nodded shyly, nibbling on her lower lip.

"Show me," I demanded, pulling on my shorts until they were halfway down my thighs. "How much do you want me?"

My hard cock hit the air, straining upward to meet her. She glanced down at me, where her hand was grasping my thick length. I didn't see hesitation in her expression but lust and almost amazement.

"I'm going crazy." She sighed, dropping my heavy cock so it smacked softly against my stomach. She sat up and pulled her panties off entirely, tossing them to the floor. "I want you so bad, Aiden." As she spoke, her legs straddled my hips once more, and good God—her slit was positioned right over my length.

I reached down with both hands and pulled her glistening lips apart with my thumbs. She was wet, just as I was hard, but I thought she could use more buildup. It'd be easier that way, and we wouldn't have to worry about there being any pain. With my thumb, I rubbed circles on and around her pink clit where it was peeking out. Her hips jerked involuntarily as she practically rode my finger. It wasn't until I could feel her slick juices running down my shaft that I deemed her ready.

Holding her steady a few inches above me with one hand, I guided the head of my cock to her entrance with the other. Her core was so hot, so wet and inviting. It took all my willpower to not thrust right in and claim her roughly. She threw her head back and moaned at the feeling of me pressed right up against her, right on the cusp of penetrating her for the very first time.

"I'm going to knot you," I warned, unsure if she knew what bonding really entailed. It wasn't just a normal orgasm; it was a were bonding ritual among true mates. It wouldn't hurt her; since she had were DNA, her body would be able to take it. But it would be intense.

She nodded, understanding what would happen. "Please." It came out as a whine, sounding like the perfect omega, even though she technically wasn't one. I groaned and inched my hips upward, slowly penetrating her. Her body was clenching down on the head of my cock, mimicking the tying to come. Gemma let out a quiet moan, that told me she was enjoying this as much as I was.

Her slick, tight heat was almost too much for me. I'd thought I would never get to feel anything like this again, but it would still be a first for me. My previous wife and I had never actually been bonded since we were never truly sure that we were mates. I'd never bonded with anyone before, and my pack had been struggling because of it. But with Gemma above me, my knot was already growing, and my jaw ached with the need to bite.

I rocked myself in farther until I found that barrier. Although she never specifically said the words, I knew that it was possible she was still a virgin. I placed my hands on her hips and held her still.

"This may hurt a little," I said quietly.

Her eyes were still hooded with lust as she glanced down at me. She nodded, as if knowing what would come next.

"I promise I will make you feel so good after this, my love."

Her face scrunched up and her mouth dropped open in a silent scream as I shoved my hips upward, bursting through her cherry. Once my entire length was buried inside of her, my knot was already halfway to full. There were still several inches for me to thrust without removing the knot from the tight clutch of her body, so I used that to my advantage. Gradually, I started up a rhythm of slow thrusts and looked up at her. She had that plump bottom lip between her teeth, eyes closed while I carefully fucked her. From the sounds that she was making, her pain had already turned into pleasure.

Bringing the hand that was on her waist up over the curve of her torso, I wrapped it around the back of her neck and brought her in close. When her eyes fluttered open again, I leaned up and kissed her. It wasn't perfect, seeing how distracted I was by the feel of her around me. But I still needed to kiss her, to feel her soft moans and whimpers against my lips.

"Is this okay?" I murmured, voice breaking slightly with the force of our bodies' movements.

She wantonly moaned a vague, "mmhmm" and started dropping her hips to meet my own. I couldn't have that, not wanting her to do any of the work or be in control. She was mine, and I needed to be the one taking care of her, not the other way around.

Growling, I grabbed her by the hips and swiftly maneuvered us so that she was lying under me while I hovered above. My knot stayed inside of her through the change in position, so I just started up the rhythm again. This time, there was no need to go slow or careful. I moved quickly, relying on instinct to guide my movements. With the new position, I could easily drop my lips down to her neck and nibble on the skin there in a silent promise of what was to come.

She was splayed out under me, sweet and pliant as anything. After having a taste of how she felt under me, it wouldn't be much longer before my rut would start. Sex was more incredible then I remembered—how had I gone so long without mating with her?

Gemma started letting out the softest noises—little breaths with each and every thrust of my hips. She began clenching up around me, making that tight heat of hers feel even more incredible. I knew it wouldn't be much longer and my knot would pop—leaving a short window of time for me to bite. That wasn't concerning to me, though. Instinct should take care of that, and I was more than sure our bond was strong enough for the mating mark to take.

It was just a matter of getting her to tie with me.

"Come on, Gemma," I murmured in her ear, using my commanding alpha voice. "I need to feel you come for me, baby—want to feel it."

I placed my weight on one hand and placed the other between our bodies. Searching, I found her clit once more with my thumb and began rubbing in time with my thrusts. Her quiet moans became cries against my mouth. We weren't even kissing by that point, just keeping our foreheads pressed together.

Then, it became entirely too much. Her tight heat practically throbbed around me, clenching impossibly hard around my knot. She was coming, moaning wantonly and writhing. The tightness was enough to send me over the edge as well. I growled and buried my face in her neck, teeth already aching for a bite. My knot swelled to its full size, already twitching with my release. Hot wetness flooded inside of her, and I couldn't even think—I just clamped my jaw on her neck. She gasped but didn't say a word.

A huge weight was lifted off my shoulders. It was intense and overwhelming, yes, but also a strange relief. I sunk my canines into the bonding spot right at the crook of her neck, growling involuntarily through it. She was writhing and whimpering, probably hurting, but I couldn't remove my teeth without making the bond void. Faintly, I could taste blood around my teeth, metallic and too familiar.

As soon as we were both finished and the aftershocks faded away, my vision cleared, and I knew I could unclamp my jaw. The bond was complete, leaving me hyperaware of her presence and her emotions. It was like scenting her, but without actually needing to use my nose. We were still tied, so I spent the next few minutes taking care of the wound on her neck until my knot finally went down.

After a few minutes had passed, I noticed she hadn't spoken. My heart panged as thoughts of hurting her ran through my mind. I pushed myself up onto an elbow and peered down at her. "How are you feeling?"

"That was ... intense," she said breathlessly.

Though her eyes were still closed, she held a small smile that told me she was sated. It was the mixture of emotions I could feel coming from her more strongly now because of the bond. I couldn't distinguish whether she was happy or having second thoughts.

I opened my mouth to ask her which but received my answer when she pulled me down on top of her and kissed me with such heated passion I was finding it hard not to give in. My knot hadn't completely gone down, and I could feel myself growing hard again. Every fiber of my being said to start moving inside of her again, but I fought against it.

"Baby, I think we should let you rest some. I don't want to hurt you," I said pulling away from her.

"Please, Aiden, I need you," she whined before nipping my lower lip.

I wasn't sure I should take her again since it was her first time, but she was insatiable. She began rocking her hips against mine, making it harder for me to say no. She wrapped her legs around my waist, pulling me in deeper inside her.

Something inside me snapped, and I found myself thrusting into her harder than I had earlier. My mate needed me, and I wasn't going to give in until she was completely sated.

A few weeks later we realized the possibility of her being bred was much higher than we thought. It was no wonder that she had gotten pregnant right after we bonded. I had taken her two more times that night before taking a four-hour reprieve to nap, and then I took her a few more times.

It was clear to me that Gemma had accepted the bond. I knew she had to be sore, but we couldn't seem to keep our hands off one another. It was as if she sensed my need to rut after having marked her as mine.

Epilogue

Gemma

I leaned back in the chaise and stared over the expanse of the estate. The view from the balcony was pretty incredible, as the main house was on the hill overlooking the smaller homes and the forest. As the sun set, more and more of the weres roaming the area began shifting into their wolves to hunt and run.

After Aiden and I had bonded, the pack was restored to its full capabilities. I had spent a day going through the estate, meeting everyone who had previously been stuck in their wolf form. They were all eternally grateful to have their previous freedom restored, and I was more than happy to have given it to them.

Even more so, considering the act that had restored the pack had also given me pups of my own. Pups plural. A boy and a girl, but I had just found that out earlier today. The doctor understood the special circumstances, being the go-to for the pack. With a mischievous little smirk, he had said that both babies were perfectly healthy.

I couldn't wait to tell Aiden.

I sighed as the sun dipped below the horizon, casting an orange light over the treetops. There was a low purr sounding behind me, and I knew who it was.

"Isn't it something?" I asked rhetorically. "All of this … the pack, the estate, all of it?"

He carefully lowered onto the chaise next to me, humming in agreement. "It's all ours."

Not just his anymore. We were in it together at this point.

"Did you talk to John today?" I leaned into his touch and placed my hand over his, where it came to rest over the slight swell of my stomach.

After the second and the alpha of the eastern territory were both dead, the rights to the territory became Aiden's.

He had been grappling with the idea of merging the territories for weeks until coming to the decision that it would be better to have two allied territories than one managed by one alpha. So, he decided to offer the position to John. Initially, John was shocked since he wasn't alpha material, but he understood why he was asked knowing that Aiden felt the need to be closer to me, at least until I had given birth.

"Yes. He's in although there isn't much of a pack left. Once they heard that they would have to answer to an omega, a few of them fled. Still, the majority that remain just want a leader who isn't a tyrant and manipulator, no matter what his designation is. It's just the same as when I announced him as my second in command. He was going to replace me eventually, and people didn't like it at first, but now they see how capable he truly is. He'll make a good leader for the eastern pack."

I smiled absentmindedly. That was definitely a smart idea, forming an alliance between the two feuding territories.

"So now that all of this is over, what are you going to do?"

Aiden's arms enveloped me fully from behind, and he nosed thoughtfully at the pink scar of our mating mark. "Think I'm going to expand things here, focus on the home pack for a while. Now that we've recovered, it'll be a lot easier to build the business back up. And, of course, I have my mate and pup to take care of."

There was an undeniable edge to his voice, that alpha pride from having a family who relied on him. I grinned and tightened my grip on his hand.

"Well, your pack will be happy that you've got a second in command lined up already. Even better, your second and your third."

"My third?" Aiden picked his head up and frowned down at me. "Who's the third?"

"Well," I mused. "Either your son or your daughter. Whichever one you decide." I placed a hand on my tummy and grinned. "The doctor just confirmed it; we're having twins, one of each."

Aiden's face split into a huge smile, and he laughed heavily. We were both filled with happiness at the news, ready and excited for whatever came next.

It wasn't such a bad life among the wolves after all.

John's story will continue in *The Omega and the Witch,* the second book in the Sanctuary Series which is now available on Kindle Vella. You can read the first few episodes/chapters for FREE. The ebook and paperback version will be available in May.

The Rogue and the Rebel, the third book in the Sanctuary Series is also available to read on Kindle Vella. The ebook and paperback will be available in late August.

You can also follow J. Raven on her Facebook Group, Wilde Raven's Steamy Reads. She keeps everyone posted on book updates, new releases, and events.

About J. Raven Wilde

J. Raven had spent most of her life traveling around the US or abroad, managing to find a bookstore in every city she visited. She began writing when she was a little girl, and it slowly grew into something she loved doing.

Now that she isn't traveling as much anymore, she spends her time writing steamy romance stories at her quiet modest home by the lake.

Connect with J. Raven Wilde

If you loved this story, sign up to receive J. Raven's newsletter at www.TwistedCrowPress.com. Subscribers get the latest information on cover reveals, new or upcoming releases, and promos. Plus, it's FREE, and she promises never to spam you or give out your information. You can also follow her on her Facebook Group, Wilde Raven's Steamy Reads.

Printed in Great Britain
by Amazon

47415211R00076